Snapshots

Robert Dawson
From the Great Central Valley Project

Snapshots

Glimpses of the Other California

Selected Stories by
Gerald Haslam

DMB
DEVIL MOUNTAIN BOOKS
WALNUT CREEK, CALIFORNIA

Acknowledgment is made to the editors of the journals *Main Trend*, *Cache Review*, and *Colorado State Review*, and the anthologies *The Fantastic* (Murray McNeil III, ed.) and *Home Valley* (Art Cuelho, ed.), where some of the stories in this collection originally appeared.

Gerald Haslam

Snapshots

Glimpses of the Other California

©1985 by Gerald Haslam

DEVIL MOUNTAIN BOOKS, P.O. BOX 4115, WALNUT CREEK, CA 94596. ALL RIGHTS RESERVED.

Design and Cover / Wayne Gallup

LIBRARY OF CONGRESS CATALOG CARD NUMBER: 85-061449 ISBN: 0-915685-03-5

5678 · 54321

For Jan

Contents

Foreword

These stories were read in manuscript atop a high bluff looking westward across the pounding surf towards that mystic land where the Yurok sent their souls if all went well. It was a few hundreds of miles in terrestrial space and a few light years in lifeways removed from the people who populate Gerald Haslam's "other California."

John Steinbeck covered the migration westwards of their parents and grandparents; Mary Austin in her early period limned the land to which they came in romantic hues; Frank Norris made an impersonal Moloch out of the land's grain bonanza days, and Bill Rintoul preserved the lore and the lingo of the oil fields where many of them settled down and too often out. No one save Haslam has woven the threads of life that make the fabric of existence for the humans of his stories.

He writes about the Cable Tool Club and the Tejon Club and the talk and the mores and the customs of men and women and kids who have led and still lead lives by dint of "picking in short cotton," as the saying once had it. These are humans that he knows, inside, outside and on the darkest night does he know them, and, more importantly, respect them for how they act and react in the fell clutch of circumstance. It would be easy, too damned easy, to class these as regional stories, perhaps even parochial, and consign them to the literary dust bin maintained for such by the self-appointed and -anointed *literati.*

Such consignment would be a grievous error but no more so than many such committed by the *cognoscenti,* to whom the lives of which Haslam writes are as foreign as were the lives of which William Faulkner wrote before he was "discovered," as it were, by Arnold Bennett, and the lives and the land of his stories sanctified thereby. Both men wrote, and Haslam still writes, of the people and the lives and the land that they knew. The similarity ends there. Haslam writes a lean, stripped, prose that packs much of humanity into small compass and does it without diminishing or demeaning the lives of which he writes.

The stories here are, as he calls them, "Snapshots," frozen by his skill at a climactic moment of their lives at their beginning or their ending or at one of those moments in mid-passage when the past springs up so greedily that present and future are of no consequence whatsoever. These are very very human lives of which he writes and in their humanity, stripped of the artifices and pretenses of so-called polite society, we feel our own unanswered agonies. This, as it seems to me, is the hallmark of sterling writing, no matter what its topic.

W. H. Hutchinson
Chico, California

Snapshots

His Ways Are Mysterious

Glendon was gazing toward the Tehachapi Mountains after having begun irrigating that morning when, with a sudden grip of recognition, he realized that it wasn't a sunrise he was watching at all, it was God Hisself revealed in His Golden Splendor just to him. "Thou art my Prophet," he heard a voice boom. "Preach my gospel. Convert sinners. Take wives unto thyself. I wilt send thou Signs." The young man's thin knees buckled, and he collapsed like a drunkard's dreams.

When he came to, he found himself sprawled on a dirt bank next to the irrigation ditch, his shovel beside him, his billed cap knocked askew. The sun was over the mountains, and an unfamiliar lightness buoyed his body. "I cain't believe it," he whistled through his teeth as he straightened his cap. He had never been an especially religious person, although he had been marched to Sunday School throughout his childhood, so he could not understand why he had been Chose. His Ways Are Myster'ous, Glendon had often heard the preacher at the Free Will Gospel Church of God in Christ say, and it was true. It was surely true. Rising, he bathed his face in the clear water gurgling through the ditch, then turned toward the house. "I just cain't hardly believe it," he repeated.

In the bunkhouse kitchen that morning, he poured himself a cup of coffee and sat at the table, still trying to understand the Miracle that had occurred. The radio was blaring country music, but it now sounded profane, not entertaining, just as everything around him looked dull after the Grandeur he had witnessed. He said nothing, and finally Mrs. Watson, who was cooking, commented, "You're mighty quiet this mornin', Glendon."

How could he tell her? He sighed then announced, "I seen God a while ago."

1

"Sure you did, honey," replied the older woman without turning. "Want some grits with them eggs?"

"I really seen Him. I had me one a them revelation deals."

"Sure you did," agreed Mrs. Watson, plopping two fried eggs like the greasy eyes of a hanged man onto his plate.

Glendon stared at the eggs—were they a Sign?—then at the woman's broad back. "I'll take some a them grits, please," he said, having decided to disclose no more about his Mission, not right now at least. He had not been told to announce his prophecy yet, so he decided to wait for another Sign.

A moment later the other two irrigators, Manuel and J.R., strode into the room, poured themselves coffee, then scooted up to the table. "How they hangin', Glendon?" grinned J.R. The Prophet winced at the implied profanity, and J.R. seemed to interpret his expression as a greeting.

"Ola Flaco," grinned Manuel.

"Say, Miz Watson, you sweet thang," called J.R., "when you gonna break down and step out with me?" He winked at Glendon and Manuel. He was a rough cob, J.R., and a womanizer, who seemed to take pleasure in pushing others. Glendon was always uncomfortable around him and his aggressive, mocking ways.

"When I get that desperate," the elderly woman parried without turning, "it'll be time to put me in one a them old folks homes."

The irrigators laughed, but Glendon remained silent. What would be the next Sign, when would it come?

"Que pasa, Flaco?" asked Manuel.

"Oh, nothin', but I'm gonna take some wives unto myself."

J.R.'s brows raised. "Say what? *Unto* yourself."

"Some *wives*?" asked Manuel, smiling.

Glendon nodded. Maybe he shouldn't have told them.

"Well, I hope they're better'n that wart-hog you took unto the dance last Saturday," grinned J.R. who always seemed to accompany the prettiest ladies.

No, he shouldn't have told them. They weren't ready. He'd wait for a Sign. Just as he finished eating, Mrs. Watson said, "When you're done, honey, I got a grocery list for you. Take the pickup into Arvin."

Becoming a Prophet had not lessened Glendon's appetite. He engulfed a second serving of biscuits ladened with bacon gravy. "I swan," clucked Mrs. Watson, "if you don't eat for two, and slim as you are! If I's to eat like you, I'd weigh a ton."

"Instead of half-a-ton," whispered J.R., and Manuel nearly fell off his chair. Not dignifying the remark with so much as a smile, Glendon stood. "Well, I gotta go get them groceries so's I can be back in time to change my water," he announced, the tone of his voice informing J.R. that he would have nothing to do with such comments. Taking the pickup's key from its hook, Glendon moved with detached dignity, his eyes scanning for a Sign.

"What's wrong with him?" he heard J.R. whisper to Manuel.

After a pause, Manuel replied, "Loco in the cabeza," and they both laughed.

"Leave the boy be!" hissed Mrs. Watson, and the two men quieted, still grinning at one another, while Glendon climbed—slowly and gracefully as a Prophet should—into the battered truck and clattered away toward town.

His market cart was loaded with supplies when he approached the checkstand and, as usual, picked up a copy of *The Enquirer* to scan while he waited for the clerk to check his groceries. The headline immediately leaped at him and he all but staggered; he didn't know what it meant, but it was clearly a Sign: "SIAMESE TWINS FACE FIRING SQUAD: One Brother Guilty of Murder." It was like they were the only words on the page; all the other print could have been gibberish. His chest tightened and he gasped.

"You buyin' that paper or rentin' it?" asked the clerk.

"I'll take it," the Prophet replied huskily. Even his voice was changing, he sensed, deepening in response to his new role. "Did you read that deal about them two brothers that're stuck together and one's gonna get shot?"

"Huh?" the lady replied, not looking up.

"Well, they're just like me and you, stuck unto sin."

3

The words came out of him without thought, as though some Greater Voice spoke through him.

"Thirty-seven eighty-eight," she said with a tired smile.

"Verily I say unto you. . . ," the Voice spoke through him.

"There's other people waitin'." The woman's eyes narrowed and so did her tone.

"Oh," Glendon said. He paid quickly and carried the groceries out to the pickup then hurried back to the ranch. He would teach them, all of them. He would spread the Word.

As soon as he had arrived and unloaded the groceries, Glendon hurried to his cabin where he read and reread the mystical article, the Sign. Finally, remembering that he had to change water on the sugar beets, he stood and headed for the door. On his way out, he spied something moving on the brass doorknob that the boss had installed when he had lived in this very cabin years before, and that Glendon kept polished. Squatting and squinting, he realized that it wasn't a bug as he suspected, but a curved reflection of his own angular form, yet there was more: next to him, attached like a swerved shadow, was a dim being, ominous and vaporous. He recoiled and swatted at it, but hit nothing; it was incorporeal and could not even be seen except in the polished brass.

Staring at the image once more, he noted that a tiny wizened face stared back at him, and that the thing itself was small, just the vestige of an evil twin and that, Glendon realized, was why he had been Chose; he had his own evil twin under control, squeezed down to a nub. The evil face in the doorknob was surely the next Sign: folks're all stuck unto sin just like the mystical voice at the grocery store had said, and they gotta get shed of it to enter the Kingdom. He, Glendon Leroy Stone, had been Chose to spread the Message because His Ways Are Myster'ous, His Wonders to Behold. Glendon beheld himself and his pitifully shrunken evil twin once more in the knob then hurried to the sugar beet field.

At lunch the Prophet kept his Message to himself because J.R. would make a joke out of anything. He realized that he should start converting the people nearest him before Spreading the Word, but couldn't figure how to avoid J.R.'s sharp and taunting tongue, so he sat tensely at the table, barely able to finish his second helping of chicken and dumplings, when J.R. suddenly jumped up and exclaimed: "Hell's bells! I forgot the water on the milo!" then sprinted out the door, leaving Glendon and Manuel alone at the table. His Ways Are Myster'ous.

The Prophet immediately faced the remaining irrigator and asked: "Do you believe on the Lord Jesus Christ?"

Manuel, whose mouth was full, mushed, "Humph?"

"Have you been washed in the Blood of the Sheep?"

"You mean the Lamb?" Manuel asked.

"The Lamb?"

"Hey," Manuel said, "I been baptized. I been confirmed. I go to mass every Sunday. How 'bout you, ese, I never see you goin' to church."

Glendon did not dignify Manuel's smirk with a reply: he had been Chose and that was that. Then the Voice spoke through him: "Verily I say unto you, we are all born as twins, Good and Evil, stuck unto one another, and to enter unto the Kingdom, we gotta get rid of the Evil half."

"What?"

"The only guy born without this evil twin deal was Jesus Hisself!"

Manuel's brows knitted and he put his fork down. After a long pause, he asked, "What about the Blessed Virgin Mary?"

For a moment the table was silent, then Glendon responded: "She wasn't a guy."

Something in Manuel's eyes changed as he agreed, "That's right, she wasn't."

Glendon felt Manuel's gaze, felt it as he never had before. There was something new in it, something like respect. "Ain't you never felt the dark take you over like whenever you're drinkin' beer or whenever you're with a woman? Ain't you never just been *took* unto sin?"

Manuel's gaze appeared troubled. "Maybe," he conceded.

"Well, that's whenever your bad twin's takin' over, and if your twin goes to hell, *you go too because you're attached.*"

"Where'd you hear all that?" Manuel's voice cracked and within Glendon something swelled. The other man's eyes were troubled and, for the first time in his life, Glendon felt as though he had the power to influence someone else's mind: the Power of God Revealed.

The Prophet stood, feeling stronger than he ever had, carried his dishes to the sink, then strode to the door, calling over his shoulder, "Believe on the Lord."

"I do," he heard Manuel stammer. "Swear to God, I do."

If he did, J.R. didn't. "What's this religion deal ol' Manuel's tellin' me about?" he demanded at breakfast the following morning.

"Well, I'm fixin' to preach the gospel," Glendon stammered, not wanting to face the other man's disdainful eyes.

"You?"

"I been Called," Glendon mumbled.

"Oh yeah," grinned J.R., and even Manuel smiled. It was clear that J.R.'s evil twin had took over.

For a moment, the table was silent except for the smack of meat being chewed, and Glendon felt their gaze heavy on his hot face. Finally he glanced up and, just as he did, J.R. stood with an odd expression on his face. He said nothing, but pointed at his gaping mouth, then dashed to the sink and tried without success to drink. He began hitting his own chest, his eyes all the while panning wildly around him.

"Hey, he's chokin'!" Manuel said, and he jumped up and began pounding the other man's back.

Mrs. Watson emerged from the pantry and asked, "What's wrong?"

J.R.'s face was darkening and he began swinging his arms like a man in a fight. Manuel ducked, calling "Hey!"

Not knowing what else to do, the Prophet rose and, fearing that J.R. might accidentally hit Mrs. Watson, he

moved behind the choking man and grabbed him, firmly
pinning his arms. When he squeezed, J.R. made a coughing
sound and a bullet of beef shot from his mouth. He collapsed
in Glendon's grasp.

"Oh, God! Thanks Glendon," J.R. finally gasped after
being helped into a chair. "You saved my damn life! You
saved my life!"

The Prophet stood there comforting the toughest guy
he'd ever known, and through his head one message passed
and passed again: His Ways Are Myster'ous.

"Don't thank me," he told the relieved man, "thank
God. It was Him give me the Power." He had not only
squeezed the chunk of beef from J.R., he had given the
man's evil twin a good crushing too.

"I'll do it," J.R. assured him. "I'll surely do it."

Glendon noticed how the other man was looking at
him, the obvious admiration, and he noticed that Manuel
said nothing. He realized that he had brought into the Fold
the two worst sinners he knew, maybe the two worst in Kern
County. Why, the devil was easy to beat when you were
Called; there was nothing to it. And he could tell that Mrs.
Watson, a good Christian woman, now understood his Mission. She placed one hand on his arm and said, "That was a
wonderful thing you done, honey. You'll have the highest
seat in Heaven."

Well, maybe he *would*, Glendon realized, maybe he
just would, but to earn it he would have to take his message
to the World, show them his perfection as a kind of model
deal. As he shoveled mud from rows that day, and patched
up leaking ditches, he considered how he would begin
spreading the Word. He had, of course, seen *Watchtower*
sellers lining Arvin's corners on early mornings, all dressed
up and grinning like street whores. They chose the right
places, but they just *stood* there. Glendon would do them
one better.

He dressed Sunday morning in his almost-new J.C.
Penney suit. His boots were polished and he wore a necktie
Mrs. Watson had given him for Christmas. He splashed on
plenty of aftershave too. When he walked to the kitchen to

fetch the key for the pickup, which he had permission to use, J.R. called, "This ol' boy smells like a French cathouse. Watch out women!"

"You oughta be goin' to church with Manuel," the Prophet advised.

"Sure," grinned J.R.

No doubt about it, Glendon admitted, J.R.'s evil twin had took back over. He wouldn't be grinning if that meat was still stuck in his throat. Well, today the Prophet had other tasks, but he would Save that sinner once and for all, and soon.

In town, Glendon stationed himself on the corner of Bear Mountain Road and School Street, where most church-goers would have to pass, as would the early morning beer bar habitués. He stood quietly, hands clasped behind his back, waiting. Two small Mexican children, a boy and a girl holding hands, passed on their way to the Catholic church. "Do you believe on the Lord?" he asked with a smile. They glanced at him, then hurried on without replying.

Before the Prophet could become discouraged, a disheveled man approached walking in the opposite direction—heading, Glendon guessed, for that row of beer bars known locally as Tiger Town. Here was a sinner if ever he had seen one, the evil twin practically obliterating what-ever remained of the good one. "Have you been washed in the Blood of the Lamb?" Glendon demanded. He could not mince words with sinners.

"Huh?" The thin man wore an old baseball cap at an askew angle with its bill pushed up so that he resembled in profile a duck with a broken neck.

"Have you been washed in the Blood of the Lamb?"

The man's rosy eyes seemed to throb as he examined the Prophet. "I ain't even had a shower. You can't loan a guy a buck for breakfast can you, pal?"

The old boy looked vaguely familiar; perhaps Glendon had once worked with him. In any case, he wasn't giving money away. In fact, he might just *collect* some like those TV preachers did, an idea he had been playing with. Feed the Hungry flashed into the Prophet's mind just as he started to say no. He realized that he was being Tested: His Ways Are Myster'ous. "You mean you haven't eat?"

"Not for days, pal."

"Well . . . here." He handed the man one of the trio of dollar bills he carried. "You *do* believe on the Lord, don't you?" he asked, but the man was already shuffling away.

"Sure thing," Glendon heard the unkempt man call over his shoulder, duck's bill bobbing toward Tiger Town.

Uncomfortably, the Prophet watched his dollar clutched in the man's hand disappear into the doorway of the Nogales Saloon. He wasn't certain they served breakfast there, unless the man favored pickled eggs and beer nuts, so Glendon continued staring at the distant doorway, half expecting the man to emerge in a halo of light and raise his hands toward Heaven in thanks for his meal. He knew this had to be a Sign, not one of those drunk-begging-money deals. All he saw, however, was two more men—one well-dressed and wearing a vast white Stetson, the other bareheaded and tattered—slip inside the doorway. He was tempted to walk right down there and challenge those sinners, even if they were only eating breakfast, when he felt a tug at his sleeve.

He turned and faced a pale young woman—not much more than a girl—dressed in a green gown, who extended a rose wrapped in wax paper. "Peace my brother," she murmured, smiling gently. "Won't you buy a flower for God's love?"

"A flower?" Maybe this was a Sign too.

"For God's love."

"Well, I been washed in the Blood of the Lamb."

"Won't you buy a flower?"

"How much?"

"God sets no price. Your love offering will suffice." She was a very pretty lady—her evil twin didn't show at all—and Glendon had not forgotten that he was to take wives unto hisself, so he withdrew a second dollar bill and handed it to her, then accepted the flower.

"Thank you, my brother." She touched his arm tenderly. "You are standing alone. Do you wish company and joy?"

"Well, I been washed . . ."

"Why don't you come with me to meet God on earth, the Bagwan Dawn Mahwa who has come to release life's love."

"Well, I been . . ."

Her grip on his arm tightened, and she pulled him. He noticed then other green gowns stalking the streets, several with people in tow. "Come my brother, to the earthly paradise where all is love and no needs go wanting."

Glendon jerked his arm free. "Hey," he said, "I don't think you believe on the Lord Jesus."

"He was a great teacher, like the Bagwan Dawn Mahwa who has succeeded him. Come to the new paradise. Join us. Join us." Again she gripped his arm.

"This ain't one a them *goo-roo* deals is it?" he demanded.

Although the girl had given no visible signal, Glendon could see three other green gowns heading purposefully in his direction, and he sensed that they were reinforcements, so he hustled away after freeing himself from her grip, away toward Tiger Town where he thought she was not likely to follow. As he passed the Nogales Saloon, he heard harsh laughter and another girl in one of the green gowns fled, red-faced, out the door. "Where you goin', baby?" he heard a rough masculine voice call after her.

It's all different kind of sinners, he told himself as he stopped just beyond the saloon.

Glancing down the street, he noted that four green gowns were now heading in his direction, while one was scurrying the other way. Well, he knew a haven when he saw it, so he dashed into the Nogales's darkened interior and hurried to the bar's far end, then slid next to a guy—the same one with a crooked cap, the Prophet realized immediately—who was drinking his breakfast and, as it turned out, Glendon's dollar. Well, at least the old boy might keep them goo-roo deals away, the Prophet figured.

10

The red-eyed man turned and asked, "You ain't got a smoke do you, pal?" He seemed unperturbed to find his benefactor seated next to him.

"I already *give* you a buck," Glendon pointed out indignantly. No doubt about it, he thought, this old boy is clean took over by his evil twin.

"No smokes, eh?" He sure looked like someone Glendon knew, but the Prophet couldn't name who.

Just as Glendon was about to snap a response that would shock this old sinner onto the Path of Righteousness, the thick-armed bartender said, "What'll it be?"

"Oh, gimme a beer," said the Prophet. He pulled his final dollar from his pocket.

"Comin' up."

"You wouldn't wanna buy me a refill, would you, pal?" asked the old drunk.

"I *already* give you a dollar," Glendon hissed.

No green gowns appeared and the Prophet was drinking his draft with relief when he glanced at his image in the fancy mirror behind the cash register, a Man of God sitting next to a common drunk and slurping the devil's brew. His face warmed and reddened, his stomach suddenly churned, so he turned to the old boy and demanded: "How's come you to drink beer with that dollar I give you for breakfast, anyways?"

The red eyes faced him and he heard the man croak, "You *give* me the buck, so mind your own damn business!"

Glendon sensed that he had this sinner on the run. After he finished his beer—no sense wasting it—he really told him: "You got no business takin' folks' money that works hard for it. You're pullin' one a them beggar deals when you oughta be out workin' your ownself. Evil's flat took you is what's wrong and unless you wash in the Blood of the Lamb . . ."

For a second, Glendon didn't realize what had happened—the sudden shock—and by the time he did, the old boy had socked him a second time and was grappling with him, had him down in fact. He was strong for a skinny old weasel, or something was weakening Glendon, because the drunk—cap still firmly awry on his head—had the Prophet pinned to the floor while the saloon's other patrons laughed and shouted. Above him, Glendon registered only the flaring eyes and ghastly face of the man like sin itself.

It was humiliating because no matter how the Prophet bucked and surged, the old drunk stuck to him, and the laughter of those other drunkards burned his ears. Determined to teach this sinner a lesson, Glendon sucked in his breath for a decisive burst when, suddenly, he recognized the face snorting above his: it was the very one he had seen in his brass doorknob that first day, his own evil twin's, and that dark brother had him now as surely as Cain had Abel. Glendon Leroy Stone began to pray as he never had before.

That Constant Coyote

Agreed, water ouzels dance through the mad music of mountain streams. . . .

Agreed, quaking aspens disintegrate in wind. . . .

Agreed, I never was what I used to be. . . .

Agreed. Agreed. Agreed.

But don't tell me what's done's done. I've lived too long and held the sticky hands of too many grandchildren, stood watching day slide into earth like a sharpened shovel while our generations clasped. I've gazed ahead into a past as jagged as the crazed castrato calls of evening coyotes. My own coyote, the very one whose song had haunted my sleep as well as my stock—only days after a state hunter had poisoned him and buzzards had disrobed his bones—appeared this morning in triplicate, gloriously alive, from a den above our high pasture on Brekenridge Mountain: the same flesh multiplied, pups probably wiser because of their father's recent fatal mistake. Despairing for my feathers and my wool, I welcomed the old scamp back, even tripled. State hunter be damned. Age teaches you to appreciate characters as much as character. I'd missed the quality of our continuing contest. In fact, I'd been missing a lot of things recently.

I watched my multiplied nemesis pounce on bugs and, one third of him anyway, trap then lose a mouse. You're young again, old timer, I thought, you'll learn. You'll nail the next one. I observed him wrestle himself down an embankment, snapping and yipping while young momma coyote—the old scamp always did favor youthful consorts—trotted heedlessly ahead past a stand of aspen, scanning for breakfast.

Finally the quartet—momma in the lead—bounded out of sight into an arroyo near Bear Creek, and I hiked back to my pickup, swigged a shot of pain killer, and headed home, satisfied that in this remote region, at least, the eternal

13

struggle would be renewed. Bouncing back toward breakfast, I couldn't help but chuckle at the irony of it all, my genuine joy at seeing the old lamb stealer after all the cartridges I'd wasted trying to plug him.

Damn his old carcass, but every spring it seemed he'd lose his taste for mesquite berries and mice and garter snakes, and commence cropping my sheep. Every spring, about two lambs in, I'd lose my patience and whistle a few 30-30 protests toward him. In fact, I don't know if I ever really wanted to ventilate the pirate, and it was my son who had called the state hunter. After a few seasons I'd finally figured out that the old boy had to be feeding his own youngsters that lamb, the same way I was feeding mine. He needed a better food source for those fuzzy bundles than the spring rodent crop provided. I became more tolerant then, a tad more.

Most of all, I've come to admit that I liked the mangy old coyote, with his desire for young sheep and young lovers. Once, long before this damned disease got me, my son and I were visiting the redwood grove where we've kept our family camp for nearly a century; I was reading, my boots propped up on an ancient stump, while the horses blew and my kid cooked coffee. All of a sudden I sensed eyes on me. I figured it had to be the mystery story I was enjoying, and chuckled at myself. A minute later Len, my son, whispered, "Would you look at that."

I looked. Not fifty yards away on the edge of a clearing sat the old boy staring in my direction. "He probably checked at the ranch to make sure we left our rifles home," I told Len.

"Then trailed us," he added.

"He probably just figured this was a stag party and followed us all the way up here. After all, he *is* a senior partner in this outfit."

Len laughed and finished the coffee. I kept reading, but every time I looked up, there he sat, although once or twice I caught him snapping up grasshoppers like a bum snitching hors d'oeuvres: what a character.

The grove, with its ferns and creek and giant trees, sat in a canyon on the far edge of our property, fully ten miles from the ranch house. My grandfather had bought that corridor of land specifically so we could own it before some renegade loggers cleared those beautiful trees the way they wanted to harvest every other accessible redwood in the Sierras. At one point, he'd even posted a man there—a hard case, I'm told—to protect our timber. Over the years, several chairs had been carved out of small stumps, and one large table had been made by smoothing a large one, the remains of a titan felled by lightning. Two hollowed trees—both still living—took the place of tents; we'd been sleeping in them as far back as I can remember. We had also over the years hammered a few cabinets and boxes on snags, constructed a corral, and built a large fire ring.

There was something enduring about that place. On the stumps I could read carvings made by my grandfather and his pals eighty-some years ago, and I could imagine a lively Texan who had come to California with guts and ambition and built a small empire. He and his pals had slugged down whiskey and told lies and roughhoused in this very place when Cleveland was president, and now my grandkids and their friends were adding their carving to the stumps, their lies to the echoes.

Last month, when I returned from San Francisco after hearing that my cancer was inoperable and enduring three weeks of chemotherapy and counseling, I lit out for the grove. I had enough platinum floating through my system by then to start a jewelry store, a strange fate for a guy who even refused to wear a class ring. Moreover, although my oncologist had assured me that I withstood the effects of the toxin remarkably well, I was feeling punk. My gray locks were evacuating in clumps, and eating was no longer a pleasure. Hell of a note.

At least I was over the initial shock and depression. When the local doc had given me the bad news and urged that I travel north so that specialists at the University Medical Center could treat me, I had slipped into a sump of self-

15

pity. Brandy hadn't helped, nor had my wife's deep concern. We hadn't told the family I was dying, of course, and didn't intend to until death was just around the corner. But I had remained low until I got things into perspective.

On the day after I returned home from the Med Center, Doris and I had saddled up our horses, loaded Molly, our favorite pack mule, then we'd ridden to the grove for a weekend. It had been a good journey, with trout working the creek along which we traveled, aspen groves shimmering in the breeze, and—a real rarity—a pine marten humping along a deadfall across the water. By the time we'd arrived, we were in good spirits. That's when Doris told me, casually yet tentatively, that the state hunter had killed the old coyote.

"He *what?*" My fuse was short after all that chemotherapy.

"He poisoned that old nemesis of yours."

"Well, *that's* just great," I replied sarcastically.

She stopped and stared at me. "Clint," she said, "you've been after him for years."

"*I've* been after him. It was between us, not some damned state hunter."

"Men!" Doris shook her head and began brewing coffee.

That night I'd sat at the fire after Doris turned in. Sipping brandy, I'd looked carefully at those trees and stumps, their shadows and shapes, thinking that my grandfather, my father, my son and grandson, all of them had known or did know this place. I had never met my dad, and hadn't ever seen my granddad either—both were killed young—but we had all three shared knowledge of this grove, of that bedding place within the hollowed goliath where my dad was built who built me on a feather bed who built Len in the backseat of an aging car, who built Timmy and Karen God knows where, all of us products of the same lightning that emptied the tree. Strong stuff, brandy, my personal chemotherapy. I turned in, snuggling next to Doris in the redwood's hollow.

She was snoring. I didn't blame her. This whole damned thing had been harder for her than me, I'm sure. I only had to die. She had to live with it and with the uncertain future. My future was certain. They told me at the Med Center that I had only a matter of months, and they put me in contact with the folks at the local hospice—most of them old friends—so I was downing, along with my brandy, a concoction they gave me to dull the pain that was already invading my middle.

I snuggled there next to my best pal, but my eyes, booze and drugs dimming them or not, would not close. I gazed through the frayed branches of redwoods at more stars than generations of my kin had a right to expect. Then I heard voices. . . .

I started, jerking my head to the side and saw two figures plop on the stump next to the fire ring. Well, if trespassers wanted trouble they had it. I wasn't in any mood to reason with anyone, nor was I too keen on avoiding trouble anymore. Deciding not to awaken Doris, I crawled out of my bag, pulled on jeans and boots, then slipped on my down vest.

"What do you two think you're doing here?" I demanded in a tense hiss soon as I approached the stump. Both men smiled at me in the dark. "I asked you a question," I said.

The larger of the two turned toward the other and said, "You tell him. He's got your personality."

I heard the other one reply, "The wages of sin." They both laughed. "I'm waiting," I pointed out, in no mood to play.

"Clint," said the smaller man, "you always did have more guts than good sense."

I looked hard then, but couldn't recognize either of them, not exactly anyway. They were kids, maybe friends of Len's, but his pals would know better than to sneak up here without permission. Still, they were vaguely familiar, even in the dark and they didn't seem intent on mayhem, so I said, "You boys should've told us you were coming up. A midnight visit might buy you a 30-30 greeting."

I could see them smiling, then the smaller man said pleasantly, "Why don't you sit a spell and talk. We can't stay long."

"I didn't hear your horses," I said. "Did you hike in?" I remained a little irritated but their manner relaxed me. Besides, I figured I had enough juice left in me to take them if they got frisky.

"We didn't ride in," the larger man said.

"Hell of a hike," I said, still trying to see them clearly in the darkness.

"It's all of that," the larger man replied.

Away, far to the north, I heard a coyote cry.

"This place doesn't change much, does it, Dad?" the smaller man said to the larger.

Dad? Hell, they both looked less than thirty in that light, or lack of it.

"Did Len put you up to this?" I asked.

"Oh, in a way," responded the smaller man.

"That kid," I said.

"He's a good one," the smaller man said. "Like you."

"Like me?" This was getting silly. "Look, boys, I'm tired. Why don't you roll out your sacks and we'll talk in the morning."

"We'd like to," replied the larger man, "but we've only got a little while. We just came to tell you that we're with you in this, and that everything'll be alright. Play out your hand."

"Play out my hand?"

The coyote yipped once more.

"The years don't mean one hell of a lot, but how you live does," the larger man continued. "Lenny here didn't get much of a stake, but he did his damndest."

Before I could speak, the smaller man added, "Dad did the same. You've done a job and you're leaving good stock in that boy of yours, and his kids. We're proud of you, aren't we, Dad?"

I squatted next to the fire ring. "Let's start this all over again," I suggested, wondering whether mixing brandy with painkiller was such a good idea. I felt okay, but this conversation had me befuddled.

"You don't recognize us, do you?" asked the smaller man.

"No."

"And you invited us to stay anyway?"

"Why not?" I asked. "I learned a long time ago to trust my instincts. You two're alright, but I don't remember where we met or your names. I figured we'd shake all that out over coffee in the morning."

"We met in your blood," the larger man said.

"In my blood?"

"Did you expect us to wear sheets and rattle chains?" the larger man asked.

I said nothing, but searched—really searched—them with my eyes in the gentle darkness. The smaller man wore a uniform and not a recent one. As near as I could tell, it was a doughboy's outfit from World War I. The larger man wore jeans, a rough flannel shirt and a Mexican sombrero; he had a pistol strapped high on his waist, I realized. In the breathless night, their faces finally coalesced, finally became those in the fading photos on the mantel at home.

My granddad had been killed at twenty-nine, victim of a badger hole up on Tejon Ranch that broke his mount's leg and collapsed the big bay onto Grandpa's chest. He spit bloody froth for two days before dying in a line cabin, Grandma said. Three other vaqueros buried him in an oak grove near the cabin. Grandma outlived two more husbands.

My father was vaporized by a German artillery round in France when he was twenty-one. He had lived with my mother, his high school sweetheart, for only a week before shipping overseas to make the world safe for democracy. Momma never remarried.

Which leaves me. Somehow I survived both horses and wars, further building the cattle business Grandpa had started, Grandma had built and Momma had managed. I'm almost three times as old as my dad and granddad, and have lived to see two further generations of us raise old Ned. And now I've got this cancer, or rather it's got me.

"We figured you'd come back here just like we did. It's the center," Dad added.

Feeling suddenly relaxed with my hallucination, I nodded. "You two want a drink?" I asked. They did—my kind of ghosts.

Sunshine warmed my face when Doris poked me. "Hey night owl," she said, "I thought we were going fishing."

"Huh? Yeah, oh yeah. My kingdom for a cup of coffee." I smacked my brandy-befouled lips—ugh!—then leaned on one elbow.

She brought me a metal cup full of strong brew. "You must've really been dreaming last night. You were talking to yourself, carrying on."

"I was?"

"You sure were." Her face suddenly turned grave. "Clint, were you in pain?" Her eyes glistened.

"No, not at all." I sat up fully. "Hey, don't let it get you down, hon'. I know it's the shits. I sure as hell don't like it either, but it's out of our hands, so we can't let it ruin what we've got left."

Her hand was on my face and, with the morning sun behind her, she appeared as young as that first morning when we'd awakened in the midst of these same massive trees. "I know," she said. "I know we'll both die and so will everyone else. But it's just that we'll be separated." She did not blink, that good, brave woman who has made my life so, so . . . so desirable. Thank God for Doris. Leaving her was what I really hated.

"You know what I feel like doing?" I asked.

For a second a startled look crossed her face, then she smiled. "I thought you were sick."

"Sick, not dead."

Her smile broadened. "You know what *I* feel like doing?" she asked, unsnapping her denim shirt.

Far off, beyond our grove, above on a ridge somewhere, that coyote sang. I caught it through our pounding breath and, for an instant, a flash, I realized that I'd never before heard one call this late in the morning, then I sensed our breath, our breath, felt it.

Agreed, we hover in time like sparrowhawks in wind. . . .

Agreed, our lives have passed through redwood exclamations. . . .

Agreed, we never were what we used to be. . . .

Agreed. Agreed. Agreed.

Trophies

"Well sir, they took me outta that wreck for dead," he admitted. "Them ambulance boys just flat give up on me, but this doctor at the hospital he brung me back." Rodney emptied the cup of coffee he had been cradling. "Want another'n?" he asked.

"Sure," I nodded. "Let me get this one."

I walked to the counter and ordered two more, seeing in the mirror not only the large man with whom I had been speaking, but other men, mostly old—retired from the oil fields or broken in them and unable to work—seated in plastic booths with coffee in styrofoam cups and breakfast on styrofoam plates. Their faces were creased and sundarkened, like a collection of well-used baseball gloves, many wearing caps or cowboy hats at jaunty angles. I couldn't help noting how different this clientele was from the one I usually breakfasted with at the hospital in Oakland: no discussion of tax shelters here, not a word about racquetball or recent vintages. These were simpler, tougher men, as my late father had been, quick to laugh, quick to take offense, their passions surging like bunched muscles just beneath their surfaces. In fact, they were what I might have been had education not rescued me: there but for the grace of God. . . .

I carried two cups to the booth and said, "Here you go, Rod."

"Thanks, Larry," he grinned and winked, making a clicking sound out one corner of his mouth, a trait I recalled from high school.

High school: if anyone had told me then that I'd one day share a civilized cup of coffee with Rodney Phelps, I'd have considered the speaker crazy. I didn't imagine Rodney would share *anything* in a civilized fashion, or that he could. He had seemed more an irrational, ominous force than a person—a tornado, maybe, or an epidemic—precisely the kind of peril opportunity had allowed me to escape.

In truth, I hadn't thought about him for years—not since I'd gone away to college, I guess—but when I'd spied the large man lurching up Oildale Drive toward the river that first evening home, I'd recognized him even in dusk and had thought immediately of the accident, sensing all the while an ancient discomfort lurching into my belly. I was driving by in heavy traffic, so I couldn't stop—I probably wouldn't have anyway—but from a distance he appeared unchanged by the thirty-plus years; shoulders wide, hair dark, gaze direct and unflinching; he even wore the same costume I'd last seen him in, the one we all wore in 1950: a white t-shirt and Levis, the shirt ghostly. Briefly, I was swept back to my adolescent years and nearly allowed my car to drift into the wrong lane, into an accident of my own.

The very next evening, driving in the same direction on the same street, I once more sighted him, just a bit farther south, but still swaggering and again wearing a bright white t-shirt and Levis. I noticed this time that, below those wide, spectral shoulders, pivoted tragic hips. His walk was less a swagger, I realized, than an elaborate limp—for a moment I wondered if it was a result of the accident. Aware of the degeneration being suffered by my own middle-aged body, I was privately pleased to note that Rodney had not escaped similar disintegration.

I remembered well the times he had bullied me. He had intimidated everyone, of course, and brutalized as many as he could during those days when street fighting was a serious and honored local pursuit. One night at Stan's Drive Inn, Rodney had walked up behind a big, easy-going lunk named Dennis McGee and broken his jaw with an unannounced punch. Another time, he had cold-cocked an East High football player named Bob Meyers while Bob sat on a public toilet; Rodney was much praised for his creativity following that incident. He even won something like a fair fight against a tough little Mexican kid named Trevino who went to the Catholic high school. There were, in fact, numberless stories of his adventures in those years and I was actually present when he duked a shop teacher at Bakersfield High, thus ending his own not-altogether-promising academic career.

Rodney, whose abundant testosterone was not matched by excessive cerebrum, had also claimed to be a great cocksman during those years, and nobody argued. In truth, most of us had toadied up to him, slapping his thick back when he regaled us with tales of his triumphs at drive-in movies or deserted groves, each wishing he had been the protagonist of Rodney's yarns. It was all so mysterious to us then, so titillating, and he had more than once shown us girls' panties—his trophies, the very sight of which inflamed us—then clicked the side of his mouth.

In any case, Rod's legendary exploits and that terrible automobile accident had returned to me when I'd seen him, because he seemed to be a walking time capsule, bad hips or not. His appearance had even inspired an old, almost primal shadow of fear.

I was back at my late parents' house that week to comfort an aging aunt who now lived there and who was to undergo surgery, so it was not to be my usual one-day-in-one-day-out visit. I was making it a point to contact my few friends who remained in the area, and was even journeying to personal points of interest: the secret spot on the Kern River where I had parked with girlfriends, the church where I had been baptized, the football field where I had warmed the bench. For the first time since leaving town all those years before, I'd succumbed to nostalgia.

As a result, when I'd entered the newly constructed McDonalds on North Chester Avenue that morning, and noticed his broad, white t-shirted back hunkered over a cup of coffee, I'd resisted the antique urge to retreat and had instead approached him. "Rodney," I asked, "remember me? Larry Trumaine."

The heavy face—not nearly as youthful as I'd expected—had swung toward me, and I'd immediately identified ruptured capillaries beneath his tan skin like the red webs of spiders. After a moment, he'd grunted, "Be damned," then grinned and extended a large hand. "Set down, Larry. Set right down."

It turned out that Rod had gone to work roughnecking on a drilling rig after recovering from the injuries he'd suffered in the accident, and had traveled a good deal—Saudi

Arabia, Venezuela, Alaska—as a roughneck until, recently, he had badly injured his spine and been forced to retire on disability. Little wonder I had not seen him on any of my many brief earlier trips home. He lived now, he explained, in a trailer court on McCord Street not far from the river. "And you're a doctor?" he observed. "I wish I'd a knew that whenever I busted up my back. You might coulda helped me."

I only smiled.

His eyes narrowed and his voice lowered. "You recollect ol' David DeJong that was a year ahead of us in school?"

I nodded.

"He's a doctor now, too, a big shot at Kern General. Well he married that Jeanine Garcia that was the good-lookin' song leader. I screwed her." He clicked the side of his mouth and nodded to emphasize the point.

Dave and Jeanine were good friends of mine, so I said nothing, although my belly surged.

Rod seemed disappointed. He added: "And that Miller girl with the big jugs. . ."

"Sherry?"

"Yeah, I screwed her too, and she's on the City Council in Bakersfield. She loved my nuts."

I'd heard enough of his infantile babbling, so I shrugged and looked at my watch. Before I could speak, Rodney continued: "Mary Anne Reynolds that give the graduation speech, I screwed her lots of times. I used to go to her house Thursdays whenever her folks wasn't home and we'd have at it. She'd just beg me for it. I even screwed her that night in her graduation outfit."

I stood, my throat tightening. I *did* vaguely remember him hovering around Mary Anne in the parking lot following graduation. He had lingered there with some other losers while the ceremony went on, probably drinking beer. I started to move toward the door.

One of Rodney's large, knotted hands gripped my forearm. "I'll tell you somethin' else: I even screwed two cousins in one day. Got Marlene Hughes in the parkin' lot at

Bakersfield Junior College—remember her? Then I picked up on her cousin, that real purty one from Arvin—ah . . . Terry I believe her name was—and I nailed her that night. Boy, was she somethin': suck your damn sump dry." He again grinned, winked and clicked the side of his mouth.

His face blurred as I moved away from the booth, a force throbbing in my vitals like the surging of an oil pump. I'd seen enough of this pathetic husk of a man, heard enough. I didn't trust myself to speak, certainly not to tell him that I had married Terry. I didn't trust myself to tell him anything.

"You oughta come by the place," he winked, apparently unaware of my anger. "I even got their underpants at my trailer. I always kept underpants off the girls I got. You oughta come see . . ." His voice trailed off and he looked puzzled. "Somethin' wrong?" he asked.

"I've got to go."

"Hey, them gals was big shots and I had 'em."

"How about Leona, do you have her underpants?"

He rose slowly and painfully from his seat—his back clearly arthritic—and I retreated a step at the sight of those huge shoulders hunched toward me. "You sorry fucker," he growled, "don't you never mention Leona's name to me." His eyes narrowed.

The other customers suddenly quieted at the prospect of a little action, but I disappointed them by turning and walking away. I tried to tell myself that, at nearly fifty, I didn't need the hassle that would follow a public fight, but the truth is that I was afraid: I didn't need my ass kicked.

Leona Tedlock had been Rod's steady girl, one of the nice ones who seemed fascinated by him. He had dated her through most of their high school years. A good student, she had been scheduled to go away to college that fall after graduating—Fresno State, I think—but she had been killed in the accident. Rodney had been driving her along the levee, to that spot near the river where we all parked, when he had missed a turn and his car had plunged off the embankment into the stream. Although the water was shallow, it was also cold and swift and its bed was full of quicksand. Leona had been thrown from the vehicle and her body was never recovered. Rodney had been seriously injured.

Whatever he'd said to me that morning, I had no right to mention Leona's name just to hurt him; she had been a good person and she wasn't involved in my anger. It was small of me and I sat in my aunt's parlor that afternoon ashamed and wondering why I had spoken so carelessly. In fact, I was not much concerned by his certainly apocryphal claim concerning Terry, I told myself. Terry had a past—we all do and beautiful women are certainly no exceptions—but not with the likes of Rodney Phelps, of that much I was certain. You have to be mature about such things.

Still, the thought, the possibility however remote that his large hands had slid fine satin underpants from those fine satin hips, that her texture and smell hid within some dark drawer of his trailer, would not leave me. Surges of rage returned throughout the day and, with them, even more disturbing hints of titillation: I could neither avoid nor separate the two.

My behavior that morning also continued to afflict me. I was an educated man, and I had no business behaving so primitively. The more I thought about it, the more I wanted to leave Oildale and its tug toward old, toward raw passions, but I had promised my aunt that I'd remain until she returned home, at least two more days. I suddenly missed not only Terry and the kids, but everything life in the Bay Area represented to me: gentility, rationality, restraint.

Once the sun's heat had begun to dissipate that evening, I climbed into my running gear, needing fresh air and exercise to clear my mind and calm my soul. Out in the somewhat-less-warm evening air, I felt better immediately, breaking into an easy sweat and breathing deeply until I found myself jogging up Oildale Drive toward the river. Far ahead, almost at the levee, I saw in a streetlight's glow the apparition of a white t-shirt lurching in the same direction I was traveling; it had to be Rodney.

Shrugging off an ominous instant of fear, I decided to catch him and apologize for having mentioned Leona but, before I could, he disappeared. I knew he could only be going one place from there—the river's edge was pleasant on summer evenings—so I turned toward North Chester, then ran onto a side street that led to the levee road. In that darkness, I didn't want to run the route he had likely taken because of chuckholes and hidden ditches.

I assumed I'd find Rodney near the cottonwood grove where we all used to park, so I jogged slowly along the narrow track on the levee's top until I reached the curve where so long ago the accident had occurred. Then I noticed something almost luminous on the moonlit water to my left. I stopped and squinted to see clearly what it was.

The river must have been exceptionally shallow that year, because the big man appeared to be walking on top of it about midway out. His arms were extended, I could tell, and he was calling, calling something into the river's hiss. The poor bastard, I thought, all his big talk must have been to cover the guilt he still felt about the accident. I leaned back on a tree's carcass next to the road, fascinated by what I was seeing and troubled that perhaps my thoughtless remark might have triggered this bizarre scene.

A moment later, I heard or thought I heard a second voice over the water's sizzle. I scanned up and down the levee, then out toward where Rodney stood, but saw nothing, not at first anyway, then I noticed a figure rising from the current, something like a snag, its end shaggy with weeds. It swelled from the stream directly in front of that wraith-like t-shirt. My breath hurried as I squinted to identify what exactly was out there with him, but in that light I couldn't discern it.

Beyond the troubling scene on the water, I noted traffic passing on the Chester Avenue bridge—those lights in this darkness little different than they had been thirty years before—and the glow of Bakersfield to the south. Then I scanned back to the white beacon of a t-shirt and realized it had turned and begun moving slowly back toward the near bank.

My heart pounding, I slipped behind the stump as the big man approached the river's edge. Rodney's large body stopped suddenly only a few feet from solid ground and seemed to hover there, arms poised at first, then flailing slowly. I could see him pretty well at that distance, espe-

27

cially his shirt like a soul dancing over the glittering water. I couldn't figure what was going on so, my breath tight, I moved stealthily from behind the stump and down the levee toward the river's edge.

Only when I neared the floundering man did I realize that he was slowly sinking, his arms fighting desperately to reach shore: he was caught in a pocket of quicksand and his movement was a *danse macabre*. Rodney didn't notice me until I stood only a few feet away, then he gasped, "Help me," his voice as thick as the river's hiss. I looked for a branch to extend to him, but even as I did, something ominous as quicksand began pulling at my own hammering core, something as frigid and as old as the river and the sand. I stopped and gazed at him, uncertain what to do. In his desperation, he did not seem to recognize me, and the water was surging over his chest now, gushing around his shoulders. "Please, buddy," he begged, "you gotta help me."

Suddenly, I could think only of Terry, of what Rodney had said about her, and that I could never forget it just as I would never mention it. The wind seemed to cease and I did not move. The night itself waited.

He finally recognized me, I knew—his eyes locking on mine for a moment—but he said no more, and somehow I could say nothing to him as he looked away toward the bank near my feet. He seemed to grit his teeth and I gritted mine. Soon only his eyes were above the gush, then they went under.

In a moment his head submerged completely, the current spilling over it as it would a rock, and I could identify only the phantom white of his t-shirt through the water above the engulfing sand. Then it too was gone and the water smoothed.

Body shaking, I inhaled deeply, seeking to regain control while I gazed at the surging current a moment longer, at the patterned water below me, then realized fully what had occurred and my absolute absence of remorse. I turned and scrambled into inky darkness up the levee, down the road, then back toward Oildale Drive, running faster and faster and faster.

The Souvenir

"Do you think I could talk Myrtle into flyin'?" the white-haired man chuckled, and his wife—her own hair a shade of blue invented in a laboratory— smiled primly, still not confident of her new teeth. "That's a fact," she lisped, adding, "Baldwin ain't gettin' me to climb into nothin' I cain't climb out of." She smiled once more, her dentures even and white.

They sat in a clattering railroad lounge car, sipping coffee and talking to another couple—the man bald, the woman also sporting blue hair—while the train swept them up the heart of California's San Joaquin Valley, acres after endless acres of reclaimed desert now green as a tropical rain forest on both sides of them, the engine's silver snout plunging everyone north toward San Francisco.

"So you folks're from Bakersfield," observed the bald-headed man.

"Oildale," Baldwin corrected.

"It's the same as bein' from Bakersfield," recorrected his wife, shooting him an annoyed glance. "He always says Oildale, but it's just part of Bakersfield. Anyways, we're not original from there. We come out from Checotah in '37, me and Baldwin, just married and too young to have good sense."

"We're natives," interjected the other woman.

"Ain't that nice," observed Myrtle tonelessly. "Anyways, Baldwin found work in the oilfields and he's been at it ever since, forty-two years up till he retired last March, workin' for Shell Oil. Not like some of these youngsters jumpin' from job-to-job. *If they work a-tall.*"

"Isn't it the truth," agreed the native woman, whose teeth seemed to fit securely. "Dan just retired too. He was a salesman for Wards."

"Uhm. I bet that's inter'stin' work," lisped the new teeth.

The bald man nodded, his eyes twinkling.

"The stories he could tell!" remarked his wife.

While the women continued talking, their conversation drifting toward grandchildren, then recipes, finally to the fact that ladies in San Francisco always wore hats and gloves, the two men sparred for topics, touching on the general rudeness of the younger generation, the fact that *some people* should be forced to speak English if they want to collect welfare, let alone vote, the assurance that Muhammad Ali couldn't lace up Jack Dempsey's gloves. There was a pause, then the bald-headed man asked, "You folks get up to Frisco often?"

"Naw, not for years," Baldwin replied. "Me and Myrtle just thought, why not? It's time to travel some." He smiled and his own large, yellow teeth gave him the appearance of a happy mule. He shifted his heavy shoulders. "Yessir, why not? But do you think I could talk her into flyin'?"

The salesman's smile faded into a knowing scowl. "Well," he intoned, "you won't know Frisco. It's been taken over by beatniks and hippies. Our daughter lives up in El Cerrito and she took us over there last summer. You'll really be surprised at what's on the street."

Again the yellow teeth grinned. "Well, I don't mind if I do see me a hippie. Like I told Myrtle, I'm gonna get my pitcher took with one a them boogers for a souvenir."

His wife, although in the midst of a list of grandchildren's accomplishments, remarked, "You are not." She smiled at the other woman, raised her eyebrows, and sighed, "*That* man." The lady with the fitted teeth chuckled knowingly.

Baldwin ignored them. "Yessir," he continued, "seen some a them suckers on TV, but I never seen a real one. I'll find me one, though, and get my pitcher took."

His wife paused, glancing first at him then back toward the native woman. "I *swear*," she said. Once more the other lady nodded and chuckled.

They detrained at Oakland, bidding goodbye to their new friends whose daughter awaited with a car, then walked to a waiting bus that would carry them to the terminal in San Francisco, Myrtle scurrying ahead, pillbox hat firmly planted atop her blue hair, white gloves covering her hands. Once Baldwin had plopped into the seat beside her, he asked, "What 'uz the big rush? You damn near run to the bus."

"*You* may not mind bein' stared at by coloreds," she responded tartly, "but *I* do."

"Oh, hell, them boys wasn't starin' at you."

"Hah!" she snorted, and he patted her hand. A few moments later, as the bus wound its way toward a freeway, she observed, "You'd think we was in *Aferca* is where. The co-*loreds*! I never seen so many. Just look at 'em." Baldwin also stared out the window at the dark faces and strange costumes, examining houses and stores and cars, all of it as alien as another nation. "Ain't this somethin'," he said to himself. "Would you look at that!"

Soon the bus swerved up onto the freeway, then across the Bay Bridge, muddy water swirling far below them, and Baldwin felt his stomach lighten. His wife stared stonily ahead. "Looky at that water," he remarked, but she ignored him. He knew she hated bridges.

At the terminal in San Francisco, they gathered their suitcases—him commenting again that she'd brought enough clothes for a month—and asked the Amtrak man how to get to the Busby Hotel where they had reservations. He instructed them to walk to the front of the building and hail a cab. "How much'll that run us?" asked Myrtle, but before the man could answer, Baldwin had departed for the front of the building and, abandoned, she rushed after him, holding her hat on with one gloved hand while she caught up. "Would *you* wait!" she demanded.

They had only walked a short distance in the large building when they saw the first one, a young man dressed in Army fatigues, a pirate's red bandana around his head, and no shoes. L-O-V-E was printed neatly just above his eyebrows in green. "Looky there, Myrtle," Baldwin said, his yellow teeth exposed in a great grin, "a hippie. I believe I'll go get my pitcher took with that sucker."

His wife, who cringed from the oblivious young man, hissed, "You *will* not," and increased her pace slightly, but Baldwin stopped and followed the buccaneer with his eyes.

"*Baldwin!*" Myrtle cried, torn between the desire to escape this building and the need not to be alone.

While the older man eyed him, the pirate twice accosted people, demanded money, and received it, the donors scurrying away as though embarrassed while the young man with L-O-V-E on his forehead counted the bounty in his hand before thrusting it into a pocket, then scouted for other potential patrons. "Would you *look* at that," observed Baldwin. "Them folks're givin' him money," he grinned to Myrtle, who tugged desperately at his arm. "Come *on*," she urged.

Baldwin had to hurry to keep up with her, his eyes nonetheless scanning everything, everyone. He nearly ran into a post when a long-haired colored girl in a 1940's dress passed them. "Would you *look* at that," he remarked, but Myrtle didn't answer. Just before they reached the heavy glass doors at the front of the building, Myrtle swerved to avoid another barefooted youngster, a girl dressed in jeans and an old blue workshirt. The youngster wore flowers in her hair and no gloves. "Peace," she murmured as Baldwin passed, and he showed her his yellow teeth.

Just as Myrtle and Baldwin emerged from the building, the lone taxi they had sighted through the large glass doors, and toward which they had been hastening, pulled away. "Now what?" asked Myrtle, sounding heartbroken.

Her tone caused Baldwin to wink at her. "Oh," he observed, "I reckon there's more'n one taxi in Frisco. Another'n'll be along d'rectly." He put down the two suitcases and opened the smaller one.

"Now what're you doin'?" asked his wife, her voice still ragged.

"I'm gettin' out the Brownie so's you can take a pitcher of me with a hippie."

"You *are* not."

"I sure as hell am. I never come clean up here not to get my pitcher took with no hippie." His tone was firm.

"*Baldwin,*" her voice raised an octave, "you *are* not."

He had just removed the camera and rezipped the bag when he felt his wife's gloved hand grip his arm. "What?"

he asked, not looking up. When Myrtle didn't reply, but only squeezed his arm tightly, he glanced up, annoyed. She nodded to their left where a pale girl stood with one bare hand extended. Someone had drawn a red-and-blue star on one of her cheeks. "Got any spare change?" she asked dreamily.

Baldwin felt his wife shudder. He examined the girl, young and thin with dark eyes and hair, no make-up except that star. She wore a kind of smock over faded jeans that had brightly-colored patches on both knees. Around her neck hung a string of eucalyptus buds. "Want your pitcher took, little lady?" he asked.

For a moment the girl didn't reply, then she asked, her voice slightly less dreamy, "Do you got a quarter?"

Myrtle's grip tightened and the lines at the corners of her mouth slashed downward as though extending beyond her chin into the pavement itself. "*Baldwin*," she begged.

"Right over there by the flower stand'd be good," Baldwin told the girl. "My wife here can take the pitcher."

The girl blinked. "What's wrong with you, man? Don't you even got a dime?" her voice had hardened considerably and she edged a step away from the muleface.

"Come right on over here, little lady," Baldwin insisted, grabbing the girl's thin arm and leading her to the flower stand, dragging behind his wife, whose glove seemed welded to him. "You get right there and Myrtle here'll snap our pitcher."

"I *will* not."

"Hey man!" the girl protested, her dark eyes wide, her voice grown rough.

He thrust the camera toward his wife, who suddenly dropped his arm and hurried back to their suitcases. "Myrtle!" he called, but she refused to even turn around and acknowledge him, standing like a gloved, hatted statue facing the street. "Damn it, anyways," he said.

"Tommy! Tommy!" he heard the girl call, and he followed the line of her vision until he saw slouching toward them the same red-bandanaed pirate in Army fatigues he'd noticed earlier. The buccaneer seemed in no hurry, but when he arrived, he extended his hand. "Got any spare change, man?" he asked in a tone that sounded more like "Stick 'em up."

Baldwin handed him the camera. "Back up there by the curb so's you can get them flowers in," he said.

"Huh?" responded the pirate.

"Hey, man!" the girl seemed to moan.

"And make sure you get us in that little square," Baldwin ordered. The buccaneer blinked his eyes then backed up to the curb.

Baldwin turned to the girl. "Smile, little lady," he directed. She smiled the way a fighter does when he's caught a good right hand.

"It won't work," the pirate said.

"You never wound it," explained Baldwin patiently. "Wind that little do-dad on top. Yeah, that's it."

Again the two smiled and this time there was a soft snap. Over the photographer's shoulder, Baldwin could see his wife's blue hair and white hat like a blossom decorating the background. He retrieved his camera, still grinning and said, "Much obliged." He returned to his wife.

The pirate followed him, but the girl kept her distance. "How 'bout that spare change?"

"What spare change? I ain't got no spare change. I worked for what little I got and I need it."

The buccaneer stared at the large, white-haired man in front of him. "Okay," he said, "then how 'bout our modeling fee."

"Your what?" Baldwin stared at the L-O-V-E on the younger man's forehead.

"Modeling fee." The pirate's eyes narrowed; his jaw thrust forward.

For a moment, the old man seemed stumped and his wife hissed out of the corner of her mouth, "Bald-win, *give* 'em somethin'."

"Modelin' fee, eh?" Baldwin chewed on it like a fresh tobacco plug, and the pirate boldly stepped closer until his hand almost touched the older man. Then the mischievous mule grin reappeared: "Well, since you took the pitcher and I's in it, you owe *me* a modelin' fee."

"Bald-*win!*" insisted his wife.

"Hey man! I want my money!"

"Your money! You got some money?" grinned the hulking old man.

"Tom-*my!*" the pale girl called to the pirate, keeping her distance.

"Yessir," said Baldwin, "I never knew they paid no modelin' fees in Frisco or I'd a come up sooner."

The buccaneer's mouth hardened to a gash. "Okay, man, I'm calling a cop."

Still smiling, the old man pointed across the street. "Want a cop? There's one right over there. Hey, officer!" he shouted.

The pirate and his lady immediately fled into the terminal, eyes wide as they glanced back over their shoulders, even though the policeman didn't acknowledge Baldwin's call. "Would you *look* at that," the old man observed. "I guess they never wanted no cop after all."

For a long moment his wife did not speak, then she said slowly, "I just *hate* it whenever you act like that."

"Like what? We come up here to have fun didn't we?"

She clattered her new teeth at him, too exasperated to speak. It seemed that a cab would never arrive. Baldwin was unconcerned. Grinning, he scanned the area, the assorted cars and people, then his eyes locked onto a bewhiskered specimen wending his way toward them from the far corner. The man wore an ankle-length overcoat that sagged like an elephant's skin, and he sipped furtively from a brown paper bag. He appeared to be carrying on an active conversation with himself, complete with shouts and angry gestures. "Would you *look* at that," Baldwin said, then he handed the camera to his wife, who absently accepted it, her eyes straining for a glimpse of a taxi. She no longer cared how much it might cost. When she finally darted a glance toward him, her husband was moving toward the man in the overcoat.

"Baldwin?" she called.

"I'm just gonna go have me a word with that booger," he explained over his shoulder.

"Bald-*win!*"

So Slender a Splinter of Song

Last Saturday night we was playin' this little club in Delano that attracts mostly old folks, real country music fans not the new ones that can't tell Ernest Tubb from Kenny Rogers, if they ever heard of Ernest, and I heard this gal say to her ol' man: "So that's the real Red Holmes. I figured him for dead by now." Well, she never had nothin' on me, boys, 'cause lately *I* been wonderin' if maybe I hadn't kicked the bucket too. *Somethin'* sure as hell has, 'cause the songs don't come no more, not like they used to. It's like I lost the music inside my head or somethin', me that's been pickin' and singin' since I's a tadpole.

That same night, I's up on the bandstand a-strummin' away on old Sidesaddle, my guitar, when I seen these two cute little honeys, the kind I love to pick up on, so I give 'em a wink and they grinned at each other and somethin' inside me went all mushy, 'cause I realized they was laughin' at me not smilin', laughin' at Red Holmes. After that set I trudged into the men's room and I looked at the road map that passes for my face, at the dyed red hair, and I said, "Shit." Wasn't nothin' else I *could* say. But that's another story.

```
GIVE ME
      GIVE ME (echo)
            ANOTHER CHANCE TO START
            WE CAN'T BE APART
                  YOUR SECOND STORY MAN

TELL ME ONE MORE STORY
TELL ME ONE MORE LIE
TELL ME ANYTHING YOU WANT
      BUT
            DON'T
                  TELL
                        ME
                              GOOD-
                                    BYE
```

36

Just a week or two ago I was talkin' to Bobby Dupree, our drummer, and I told him, "They just don't come no more, the songs. I usta could write two before breakfast. Now I don't write but two a year."

Bobby, he's one of the dope-smokin' young bucks with long hair that likes to kid us ol' timers, so he ups and says: "Brain damage. Didn't you ever read what alcohol does to your brain, man?"

"Yeah I did," I winked, "I read that myself and I said, shit, I must be one smart bastard. I must be a regular ol' Einstein, 'cause I been drinkin' pretty heavy for over thirty years and I can support three ex-wives and four kids. Hell, if it wasn't for beer, I'd be writin' them damn symphonies I'll bet. Ain't it hell to think how smart I'd be if I hadn't did all that brain damage? What's your excuse, peckerhead?"

Him and me we both laughed.

I don't know if beer causes brain damage, but it sure can wreck your heart, bust it I mean. That's how I lost them first two wives. Booze and the way life was back then when my band was goin' good, all the gals and the parties and the cars. Oh, I never hit the *real* big time, but I done good just the same. Me and the boys even played the Spade Cooley Show and the Cousin Herb Henson Show too. And I wrote one song, "Second Story Man," that Earl Ellington recorded and that made it onto the charts. I had it then, and I figured I was just one step from the big time, but I never got there.

Ol' Earl he sent his manager, a bird named Shapiro, around to see me and offer me this long-term contract to play in his band and write songs exclusive for him. Well, I was settin' around this nice bar at the Bakersfield Inn that day, it dark and cool and with just enough music, the kinda classy place I really liked. I told Shapiro that no, I couldn't do that. Me and the boys had been together for four years and we figured to stick together. "Mr. Holmes," he said, real slick, "perhaps you don't understand. Earl will make you his lead acoustic guitarist. He'll record your songs. You'll be on the Louisiana Hayride, the Grand Old Opera."

"Not without the boys," I said. Wasn't nothin' else I *could* say.

His little bald head turned red and he said, "Do you mind if I ask why?"

"No, I don't mind a'tall. Them boys're my best friends. We started together and we figure to end together."

"But Mr. Holmes, this is *business* not friendship. Don't throw away this opportunity."

"Sorry, Mr. Shapiro, but if you can't see your way clear to hire the boys too, I really can't sign," I told him.

All of a sudden his voice it got real rough. "Don't try to bluff me, Holmes. I can buy and sell hillbillies like you. When Earl Ellington sends me to get a signature, I get it."

Now I'd been drinkin' beer pretty steady that afternoon but it hadn't hit me. Or at least I didn't think it had, but whenever I heard that threat I upped and socked the sucker, knocked him ass over teakettle, and I told him, "Don't come up here threatenin' me, you squirrelly little bastard, or I'll boot your bony butt all the way back to L.A."

Well, I won the fight, such as it was, but he won the war. The last thing he said to me was, "You're through in this business. You'll never work again." He was wrong. I been workin' real steady here in Kern County, but I couldn't steal a job in L.A. or Nashville or anyplace else for that matter. There wasn't no up for me. "Second Story Man" 's as far as I ever got.

```
    GIVE ME
        GIVE ME (ECHO)
            ONE MORE SLENDER HOPE
            WITHOUT YOU I CAN'T COPE
                    YOUR SECOND STORY
                    MAN

    TELL ME ONE MORE STORY
    TELL ME ONE MORE LIE
    TELL ME ANYTHING YOU WANT
        BUT
            DON'T
                TELL
                    ME
                        GOOD-
                            BYE
```

Well, wish in one hand and piss in the other is what I always say. I done good anyways, made a livin' and been treated good generally for a guy that never graduated high school. Oh, I been duked a few times at them cuttin' and shootin' clubs, but nothin' real bad. Nowadays we get a different crowd, fake cowboys and cowgirls, folks that never even heard of Kitty Wells or Lefty Frizzell. Usta be different; usta be folks knew in their guts what the songs was about.

One night, years ago, we was playin' this little joint out Edison Highway that had heavy chicken wire strung all around the bandstand so's flyin' bottles wouldn't hit you. And they did fly. I never seen such a place for fightin'. It was like ol' Madison Square Garden only rougher, no damn Marquis of Queensberry rules, no referee. That's where I met the best damn woman I ever lost.

Tommy Jo wasn't no beauty. Cute, yeah, but no beauty. She'd got in a fight with this other gal over a big bony bastard, and the bouncer'd threw her out just when I'd snuck out to the parkin' lot for fresh air and a smoke between sets. Anyways, out she come snortin' and puffin', screechin' all the awful things she's fixin' to do to that other gal *and* the guy.

We took to talkin' and she calmed down and, before I had to go back inside, she was laughin' and so was I. I told her I'd be done at 2 a.m., so why didn't we meet there in the lot and I'd take her for breakfast. Well, she showed up and we did have breakfast, and a hell of a lot more. I never was around a woman like her and it got to where I had to be with her all the time. She done things, like lick her lips with this little pointy tongue, that just drove me nuts. That body a hers was a instrument to play and we played it, no amplifiers needed. She was my second wife, the only one I really loved, but I never knew it at the time.

We'd been married about a year that night I brung Sidesaddle home. Now some a you folks don't know about Sidesaddle, my guitar, but it's famous here in Kern County. Anyways, I come home from a Saturday night job at the Blackboard with this handmade guitar that I'd took as payment for six hundred dollars I'd won playin' lo-ball with a sideman from L.A.

I come in that mornin' and Tommy Jo was waitin' up, about half-drunk like always when I left her alone, and I pulled out that new guitar. She looked it over, then asked, "Where'd you get it?"

I explained about the card game and the six hundred, and I seen her brows go up and her mouth tighten. "Six hundred!" she finally busted out. "Six hundred! We could use that money and you took a guitar. You need another guitar like a sow needs a sidesaddle!"

That next mornin' we laughed about what she'd said and I been callin' it Sidesaddle ever since. We never had no kids so it's all I got left of her. I lost Tommy Jo when she found out about Loretta, but that's another story.

> GIVE ME
>   GIVE ME (ECHO)
>   A REASON TO BELIEVE
>   YOU DO NOT DECEIVE
>   YOUR SECOND STORY MAN
>
> TELL ME ONE MORE STORY
> TELL ME ONE MORE LIE
> TELL ME ANYTHING YOU WANT
>   BUT
>   DON'T
>   TELL
>   ME
>   GOOD-
>   BYE

I seen Tommy Jo last year at ol' Bud Healy's funeral. After the service, she was standin' with Elroy, her new husband, so I waited until he'd got to talkin' with some chums, then I walked up to her and give her a smile. She smiled back and shook my hand just a tad longer than necessary, and she looked about the same, just with gray hair is all. "How's Sidesaddle?" she asked, and give me that private laugh and all of a sudden my throat softened. I seen her eyes glisten—us standing there in our Sunday best, her husband five foot away—and I faced what I'd lost.

"You look good," I said.

"For an old heifer," she smiled.

"Too bad about Bud."

"He was a nice guy," she agreed. Her eyes was workin' me over.

"Sue Ellen seems to be takin' it good," I choked.

"She's strong."

"That oldest boy of theirs is a doctor."

"I heard," she said, them eyes still glowin'. "He always was smart as a whip. Bud was real proud of him."

"He was just a baby whenever we . . ."

"Yeah," she choked, the corners of her mouth quiverin', her eyes beggin' me not to say no more.

I looked around, then said it: "Couldn't we just meet once in awhile?"

I thought her face would collapse. It took everything I had not to hold her right there in front of everyone. Tears was streamin' down her cheeks whenever she whispered, "No."

In a second Elroy had his arms around Tommy Jo and he was strokin' her hair. "She feels real bad about old Bud," he said to me.

I got snot-flingin' drunk that night.

GIVE ME
     GIVE ME (ECHO)
          A LOVER'S LONELY PRAYER
          I MUST HAVE YOU THERE
               YOUR SECOND STORY MAN

TELL ME ONE MORE STORY
TELL ME ONE MORE LIE
TELL ME ANYTHING YOU WANT
     BUT
          DON'T
               TELL
                    ME
                        GOOD-
                            BYE

I tried to write a song about it, tried my hardest, but I just couldn't come up with nothin'. The music ain't there no more.

Rider

"Ol' Jesse Stahl ride any bangtail ever foaled," the old man wheezed.

"Jesse black?" asked Charles, his grandson.

"As coal," chuckled Grandpappy, "and hard. *Hard.* Yessir, Jesse 'bout the hardest ever they was, 'ceptin' maybe Jackson Sundown. Jackson ride too. And Bill Pickett. Yakima Canutt. They ride, boy. Ain' no riders like 'em to-day."

"All them dudes brothers?"

"Colored," answered Grandpappy. "Colored mens."

"Damn," exclaimed Charles, "I never see *them* in no movies."

"One time me and Jesse, we at Pendleton and he clownin'. Come time for saddle broncs, and he cain't find his boots, so he wear these floppy ol' shoes he clown in. They so big he cain't fit 'em in the stirrups, so he tell the boys to jam them devils in for him. This white buckaroo, he say, 'But what if you gets bucked off? You be killed.' Ol' Jesse he look dead at the boy and he say, 'I ain' gon' *get* bucked off.' He right. He work that horse till it ready to drop. I ridin' pick-up, but he cain't take his feets outta them stirrups, so we have to cut the saddle loose to get him off. Jesse he look at that white boy and he grin: 'What I say?' he ask him. Me and Jesse, we cut some rusty capers together," the old man continued, his red-rimmed eyes drifting, floating on his face for a long moment. "Ol' Jesse," he sighed.

"Stop it, Pappy!" snapped his daughter. "Them old days don't put no grits on the table. Leave the boy be. Don't give him no crazy ideas."

The old man said nothing more. He tightened within himself for he was hot, damned hot, but he resolved not to fight in front of his grandson. The boy had seen enough of that. Later, when Charles had gone out, Grandpappy cornered Joletha: "Looky here, girl," he growled, "don' you never talk to me like that again in front of the boy or I go up longside yo' head. I means it! Don' you want that boy to grow up straight?"

His daughter rolled her eyes. "Oh, Pappy . . ."

"I means it! I really means it! You a good momma, baby, but you don' know what it like for a boy to grow. That boy goin' find him some way to be a man, and I reckon what I gives him a damn sight better'n what the street give him."

Joletha ran a hand through her hair. "I don't know," she shook her head. "Those stories of yours like fairy tales. We scufflin' to eat, and you carry on 'bout cowboys 'n' Indians."

"Nawsuh!" Grandpappy wouldn't give. "Nawsuh. Ain' no play actin' 'bout it. I tell Charles 'bout workin' cattle and 'bout rodeoin'. Tha's all."

Joletha hushed him. "Pappy, don' you see it all the same for Charles? He no closer to bein' a cowboy than bein' a Indian. You gotta *see*. Them ol' days over. They *be* over."

She was right, of course, and he knew it. Oh, there were still ranches, but they were few and growing fewer. In fact, Grandpappy himself had been too late for the open range and long cattle drives, and that had finally led him to spend nearly thirty years on the rodeo circuit. When he grew too stove up to compete any longer, he had repaired to Wes Cooley's ranch at Glenville, and he'd still be riding there if Wes hadn't died, leaving the spread to his citified nephew who turned it into a summer home development. The nephew had asked Grandpappy to stay on as "a touch of the old West," but he didn't intend to be anyone's buffoon.

So he'd moved in with Joletha. He knew he could have found a cabin near Glenville and remained his own man, but there was the boy—his grandson—growing up without a father.

And Charles did listen to him, especially since the night Lonnie, the boy's main man, had been blown away on the street. Lonnie's death had deepened Charles. He spent much more time within himself. But he also spent even more time with his grandfather, and the old man gave what he sensed the boy needed, answering his questions, telling him tales, teaching him practical skills. He even managed to scratch a few dollars together so that he and the boy could travel by bus to Golden Gate Park and rent mounts. He noted with pride that Charles was a natural, sitting the horse as though born in a saddle.

But the high point came the day when Charles brought home from the library a book about Negro cowboys. Since the boy was no reader—he had left school in ninth grade, and only sporadically even glanced at a newspaper—his grandfather, a great believer in learning despite his own limited formal education, had felt matters were moving in the best possible direction, especially when Charles opened the book and showed him on a list of the outstanding rodeo riders the brief notation that proved he—a stove-up old man—he too had lived: ". . . from Langston, Oklahoma, came a bull-rider *par excellence*, Charlie 'Bo' Howard."

It flooded him with memories, glistened his eyes: the good old boys, the *hombres del Campo*, the horses and snaky bulls and the gals. Mostly it brought back Marlene, Charles's grandmother. Half-Kiowa, she could ride the wind. When she had died—Joletha just a baby—it had killed a part of him that had never come back to life, and it had probably made him a tougher rider. He just didn't give a damn after that. In Mexico he had even ridden fighting bulls.

"Who write that book?" he asked. "I never know I be in no book."

When Charles had shown Joletha, even she softened. "Your Granpappy a cowboy," she had acknowledged to the boy, and she had patted her father's back.

Two days later detectives picked Charles up for rustling a horse from the mounted police stable in Golden Gate Park. While neighborhood young bloods had cackled over Charles's feat—ripping off a pig's horse—Momma had not been amused. They had no money for a lawyer, and she was concerned that her son, juvenile or not, would be prosecuted for felony grand theft, as one city man had warned. Fortunately, the public defender made a deal, pointing out that

Charles had really just engaged in a prank, and that he had made no effort to really steal the animal, but had merely taken a joy ride. Ninety days' probation was all the juvenile judge had given the boy. Momma had been relieved at the outcome.

But Grandpappy was livid. "You don' never steal nobody's horse, nigger! Never!" The boy grinned, only to feel his grandfather pop him hard across the mouth. "Don't gi' me no sass," the old man warned. "They's things a man don't do, and horse stealin' one of 'em."

Charles could have flattened Grandpappy easily and he knew it, but he was so stunned by the old man's anger that it didn't occur to him to strike back. "Yes sir," he said.

"Ain' nobody ride with no horse thief," his grandfather explained. "Ain' nobody share they grub with no horse thief. Horse thief no better'n a re-rider. If you be a man, act like one."

The boy had rocked on his heels, undecided whether to leave this bent old man who hovered before him and return to the street brothers while he was still a celebrity. "What's a *re*-rider?" he'd finally grumbled.

"A re-rider? That what we calls all them boys what holler for extra tries at the rodeo," the old man explained. "You know, carryin' on 'bout how they wasn't ready or some such. Always got excuses. Low, boy, low life folks."

"Uhm," nodded Charles. He began to say something when his grandfather interrupted him to tell him about the rodeo.

"If you ready to be man, they's a rodeo up at Guerneville this weekend. I save a little money so's you can go and watch some riders work, and I buy you somethin' too." Grandpappy shuffled to his drawer and returned with a large shoebox. When he opened it, Charles saw a bright new pair of cowboy boots. "These workin' boots," Grandpappy explained, "the kind real riders wear. They go with that sombrero I buy you. Maybe you ready for 'em."

They spent that afternoon talking about bull riding, the techniques and tricks Grandpappy had learned during his years in the arena. He told the boy of his failures and his triumphs. "One time this bull name Screwtail he throw me, then he worry me till he knock this eye out," Grandpappy said, pointing at his drooping left eye. "Then ol' Manny Rojas, he put it back in and carry me to the hospital. That way back in '28 at Clovis, New Mexico. A mean damn bull. Flat snaky."

"Knock your eye out?"

"Clean out."

"Damn!" exclaimed Charles.

"Double damn. But I ride that rank Screwtail a month later at Flagstaff," Grandpappy chuckled. "He a bad bull though."

"Damn," the boy repeated.

Saturday Charles caught a ride as far as Cotati with one of Momma's friends, then hitchhiked to Guerneville. A Volkswagen with three long-haired young white men picked him up and they shared a joint with him as they drove. They dropped him on the road next to the parking lot and small arena nestled in a wooded canyon. There was no town visible, though cars were streaming into the lot, and large numbers of people wandered up the road from the direction he had not traveled. The people were an oddly mixed lot, not at all the John Wayne-Gary Cooper-Clint Eastwood types he had expected. Oh, there were plenty of what could be called cowboys, lean mostly, and white, sipping on beers or pulling on bottles hidden in paper bags, but there were also large numbers of hippies smiling and carrying on. Although he saw a few other black people, he felt suddenly alone, very alone. He knew no one here, and this wooded canyon was no Golden Gate Park snuggled in the comfort of his city; this was the sticks.

"Lookin' for somethin'?"

Charles turned to face a white sheriff, and his belly swooped. The pig didn't smile. "What?" asked Charles.

"You look like you're lookin' for somethin'," explained the sheriff. "Late entries sign up at the van over yonder." The uniformed man pointed toward a mobile home parked near one wooden grandstand, and Charles saw a short line of cowboys waiting in front.

Snapshots

"Thanks," he said warily.

"Good luck," winked the sheriff as Charles walked toward the van, and the boy realized the pig had seen a rider, not a nigger. Alright, he thought. *Alright.*

He joined the line, his eyes averted, and he was again surprised as several of the others waiting greeted him as though they knew him. Next to him a pimply-faced boy sporting an enormous black hat nervously fingered several crumpled bills. "What're you entering?" the kid asked Charles.

"Ah . . . novice bull riding." Saying it aloud made it real. He would indeed do what he had only been considering. There had been no talk at home of him riding, but within himself he needed to try, to find out who his grandfather really was.

"I'm gonna go in calf-roping and bulldogging, novice," the kid told him. "I'd try bull riding, too, but I ain't got enough money."

"Money?"

"For the entry fee."

Charles gulped. "How much it cost?"

"For novice events, five bucks per."

Charles had six dollars and change in his pocket. That left him eating money anyway. He smiled.

"Where you from?" asked the other novice.

Hesitating, Charles answered, "Glenville."

"Glenville? Where's that at?"

Because he didn't know for certain, Charles merely replied, "South." It seemed to satisfy the black-hatted kid.

After paying his entry fee, the other boy turned towards Charles and shook his hand. "Take 'er easy," he said.

Handing the beefy, red-faced man who registered entries five dollars, Charles said, "Novice bull ridin'."

The man took his money and began filling out a form. "You put in some practice ain't you, son?" he asked. "We don't want any of you boys gettin' hurt."

"Yessir."

"Name?"

48

"Charles . . . Charlie Howard," he quickly improvised, and the red-faced man looked up at him, searched him it seemed.

Then he handed Charles a piece of white cloth with the number N-27 printed in black on it. "Wear that on your back," the red-faced man instructed. "There's safety pins in that box. And Charlie," he said, and the boy looked at him, "good luck."

After checking the schedule of events posted on the mobile home's side, Charles wandered to the refreshment stand, bought a hot dog and coke, then leaned on one end of the grandstand to eat. Sensing eyes on him from the passing crowd, he was immediately pulled toward that storm of discomfort that often swept him when he left the certainty of his neighborhood and found himself in what he considered the white world. Glancing furtively for somewhere else to eat, he noticed a small blonde girl wearing a fringed cowboy hat approaching him followed by two adults. She stood directly in front of him so he could not avoid her, and he stopped chewing.

"Can I have your autograph?" the little girl asked, handing him a program. He was stunned, having forgotten that he'd had his number pinned on by another novice. He nearly dropped what was left of his hot dog while signing her program. The parents both smiled at him as they left.

He understood then why people gave him a second look: he *was* a rider. Why not? He pushed his straw Stetson back farther on his head and smiled at passersby, feeling easier. Then he heard a somehow familiar voice: "Say brothah!" He turned to face a small, rugged-looking black man dressed in expensive western clothes.

"What's happenin'?" Charles ventured, uncertain.

"Alright, brothah," replied the man, "Alrighty. I'm Boise Jones." They shook hands. "You new, ain't ya? Wanna taste?" The man extended a paper bag from which he had been sipping.

"No thanks."

Charles decided immediately that this was not a man to bullshit, seeing the ridged eyebrows, the askew nose, the gold teeth, the gnarled hands. "This is my first rodeo," he acknowledged sheepishly.

"Alright. We all gotta start, bro'. Who you been ridin' with?"

"Well," tempting lies crossed his mind, but Charles decided to stick with the truth, "I just ride a little in the city. My people be ranch folks, but I come from San Francisco." As they talked, other experienced-looking cowboys and gals hailed Boise Jones as they passed: "Hey, Boise!" "Catch ya for a snort after while, Boise!" "How they hangin', Boise?" Jones smiled and nodded and called out friendly greetings.

"Shit, bro', they's all kinda good cowboys come from big cities. What you enter?"

"Bull riding."

Boise Jones removed his hat, wiped his forehead, then replaced his hat. "Whew! You sure pick a pisser to start with. Whyn't you switch to somethin' else, just for a start I mean?"

"I can't."

"It's your booty, blood, but if you want some help, count on ol' Boise. First time the worst." The older man shrugged and smiled. "I gotta make it. Lemme know if you want help. Sure you don't want a taste?"

"No, man," smiled Charles. "Maybe after."

"Maybe we rub this on your *outside* after," laughed Boise Jones as he swaggered off toward two blonde women in tight jeans who had just smiled as they walked by. Charles's eyes followed the cocky figure until Jones disappeared, arm in arm with the women, into the crowd.

When he saw the bull he'd drawn—young and small by rodeo standards, but awesome to him—he wished he could disappear into the crowd as Boise had. A thick-shouldered tan beast, the bull was fully rigged when Charles climbed to the top of the chute as he'd seen the other three novices do, and looked down on the back he had to straddle. He froze there until he heard a voice—"Come on, son, you'll be alright"—and looked into the eyes of the red-faced man who had registered him.

The man smiled, and Charles managed to force a smile, then lowered himself onto the thick back, sensing power like that which had so astounded him the first time he had mounted a horse. This time, though, no saddle sat between him and the animal, so every twitch of the bull's thick muscles twitched Charles, filling him with the impression that he sat on moving, liquid metal. He perched wide and low on the bull, afraid to place much pressure on it, but the animal seemed to accept him passively. "Tighten up them knees," advised the red-faced man.

"Not that way or you get your hand caught," barked Boise Jones, whose brown face hovered suddenly near him, as Charles wrapped his grip—wearing a glove loaned by one of the white novices. "Pull that line through there. Yeah, that's it, now over. You got it, bro'." Charles could not clearly see the dark mask that instructed him through the chute rails, but he listened.

Another face popped in front of his, this one painted a ghostly white with a red nose and blue slash mouth. It wore a small derby hat perched on top of the orange-wigged head. "Don't worry, boy, I'll keep this rank bastard off'n you. You just ride 'im," advised the clown.

"From Glenville, California, on Thunderbolt Two, Charlie Howard!" the announcer brayed, and there was light applause.

Beneath him the bull surged, lifting Charles as an ocean wave lifts a swimmer, and the boy jerked his legs free. "You're okay," the gateman assured. "Just gimme the nod when you're ready."

Slipping back onto the back, he was swept with terror once more and had to grip himself hard to avoid flinching. That was all the sign the gateman needed.

In the first bolting instant Charles felt himself burst from the chute, his arm and grip hand in the lead, his butt and legs in only momentary contact with the bull. Below and in front he caught flashings of animal, of fence rails, of dirt. Holding as tight as he could, he sought desperately to reconnect his butt and legs, to tighten his knees, but the force beneath him dodged and swirled so that he couldn't even breathe, only hold on and try to press himself downward.

Then, after a nauseous swirl, the bull reversed directions, and Charles sensed an electric jolt on his arm and hand, a release, a weightlessness, ended by broken slashes of motion, by bumps and shouts, by spreading numbness.

He leaned against the fence when he came to, the clown patting his back. "You done real good, boy. Real good. You sure that's your first bull? Rode 'im like a champ. Give 'im all he wanted, by God."

A gate opened, and he was urged out of the arena, only vaguely aware of the crowd's applause and the announcer's loud appeal: "Let's give one more hand to young Charlie Howard from Glenville!"

Boise Jones and the red-faced man helped him to the bed of a pickup, where he sat, still dizzy, tasting blood and feeling the cold spot where his lip was split. "Hey, Velma," called Boise, "bring me a couple ice cubes for Charlie's lip, willya?"

"Shore thang," replied a stringy woman, and off she scurried.

"You with us?" asked the red-faced man speaking directly into Charles's face.

Charles nodded. "Think so . . ." he managed to reply.

"Hell yeah, he with us, ain't ya bro'?" laughed Boise.

Charles tried to smile.

"You may not know it, son," the red-faced man said, "but you're a bull rider. You damn sure ain't no re-rider. You carried yourself out there like you been at it for a while, and I know you ain't. Didn't he do good, Boise?"

"Damn rights! I thought he maybe bullshittin' at first, Red, but the boy a rider. A *nachal*. A pure *nachal*. Where you learn all that in the city, bro'?"

Charles's head was clearing now, making sense of what they said. "My granpappy tell me."

"Your granpappy?" asked Red.

"Yeah. Bo Howard my granpappy."

"Bo Howard! Bo Howard your granpappy? Shee-it, man, no wonder, you got it in your *blood!*" Boise Jones poked Red in the ribs. "Was he a rider? Was ol' Bo a rider? Hah!"

"I seen ol' Bo oncet years ago when I's just startin' out myself, and he was already a ol' fart then. But ride! That's gotta be the greatest bull rider ever there was. I haven't heard of him for years. When did he die?" asked Red.

"Die? Granpappy?" Charles was confused. "He ain't dead. He stay with me and Momma right now. He wait for me at home."

"Bo Howard's alive!" exclaimed Red. "Be damned. Where'd you say you're from? Glenville? I'd sure be proud to meet your granddad."

Charles averted his eyes. "I stay in San Francisco. Granpappy he stay there too."

"The city?" laughed Red. "Hell, I'm from the city myself. Butchertown. Lived there all my life. We're practically neighbors. Listen, son, you got wheels?"

"Naw."

"What the Hell," grinned the ruddy-faced old cowboy, "lemme run you home whenever we finish here. Maybe I could meet your granddad: I'd be damned proud to do that."

"I wouldn't mind pickin' up a few pointers from that ol' man," acknowledged Boise Jones. "*Hell* no. I might just drive to the city with you boys my-*damn*-self."

Still vaguely disoriented, holding ice cubes against his split lip, Charles grinned sheepishly through the sudden attention he was attracting, for several other riders had joined Boise and Red and were patting his back or shaking his hand. He didn't even notice his name being sounded over the public address system: he had won novice bull riding and was being paged to collect his award, a belt buckle. Boise had to send him toward the judges' stand.

"He's gonna be a goodun, Boise," Red grunted, his eyes following the slim youth who walked away from them toward the award ceremony. "Yessir, a real goodun, maybe."

Jones nodded. "Yeah, he got it, the . . . what do you call it . . . the *style*. He ride that rank little bull like he's part of it. I never seen a purtier first ride. Stylin'! Ain't this a bitch: Bo Howard's kin and we tellin' *him* what to do."

Red nodded. "We're a couple pistols, we are."

"That there kid's the pistol," interjected the clown, who had just joined them. "He's somethin'."

Charles returned carrying the large boxed buckle, his gaze still not entirely clear. Boise Jones handed him the rumpled paper bag and said, "Here go, blood, you earned that taste."

Charles blinked and his eyes seemed finally to focus. He hesitated, then grinned. "Maybe I rub it on my *outside*," he said, and everyone laughed.

Sin Flick

When me and Wanda and Sally and Des had made those first three flicks, we never had no problems, but when Oscar told us about that dwarf, just *told us*, Wanda right away turned off: "It's somethin' strange about 'em," she said. "I don't wanna work with no da-warf." She was serious, but we all laughed.

Oscar laughed most of all. He stoked up his stogie and said, "Hey, it'll be dynamite. Am I right? You ever seen one in a stag film? Huh? Am I right? I been in this business thirty years and I never seen one."

"Hunh-uh," Wanda shook her head. "No way. I be out turnin' tricks again befo' I work with one a *them*."

"Come on, baby," urged Oscar, "you don't even have to do much in this one, just stand around and look hot."

"No way. I be back on the street befo' I do that."

"Then hit the bricks, baby," he said real agreeable, not mean or anything. "In this business you gotta have an angle. I never heard any complaints about *Woman's Best Friend* did I? And when we did *Harem* and I got the nutless guy, no complaints. Also, when we did the vegetable salesman and the lady bit, not a word. Now why break up a happy family? We're making good money."

"Naw, not me. It's somethin' strange about da-warfs," Wanda said again, shaking her head.

"Broads," said Oscar, winking at me and Des. "So what do you think, Buddy?" he asked me.

"Work's work," I replied.

"Yeah," shrugged Des.

"Sally?" he said.

"It sounds kinky," she giggled.

Well, Wanda split and I have to say I never thought no more about it. I mean, Oscar don't run no sleaze-bag operation making movies for American Legion smokers, not any more at least. Hey, his flicks are distributed to first-class theaters all over the coast. I even seen my name up in lights in San Francisco one time, my stage name that is, Rod LaRoque, so I wasn't letting him down over some little dwarf.

We begun shooting a week later in the studio Oscar rents in Pasadena. This was one of those doctor and nurse movies, so we did some background stuff that morning. Des was the doctor and Sally was his nurse. I was this sick guy that needs to, you know, make it with a dwarf. We shot the straight stuff first, then Des and Sally making it in the doctor's office, then me and Sally on my hospital bed, then me and Des and Sally in the operating room with some of the equipment.

We broke for lunch and was all sitting around eating hamburgers Oscar bought for us, when he brung in the dwarf and introduced her as Lita. She was about *this* high, but I didn't pay any real attention to her size because she was so beautiful. I just never expected that, a face like that, so gorgeous. I couldn't help staring at her, at her green eyes that seemed like they searched me and saw something.

We all said hi and tried to be friendly so she wouldn't feel embarrassed the way some new people do, and she was real relaxed. When Oscar took her to pick a costume, I said to Des, "Jeez, I never figured she'd be so pretty."

Des, that thinks he's a card, he said in this sarcastic tone: "Just another pretty face, my man, just another pretty face." Him and Sally laughed. The way he said it, and the way they laughed, I wasn't even sure they'd seen what I had when I'd looked at her. To me, she did seem like a pretty face but more, and I wasn't sure *what* more. I felt real strange because it was like maybe she'd been showing me something nobody else could see, and like maybe she'd glimpsed something in me. I could of used a beer. "Yeah," is all I said.

I didn't like the way Des was talking. It pissed me in fact, and I didn't know why. I mean, I didn't even know the dwarf, but it just sounded wrong. A minute later, when Oscar and Lita came back—her wearing this see-through gown—I got even more uncomfortable. Her arms and legs were real short and bent and her body looked like a lump of putty, but her face it took my breath away. Those eyes were emeralds. All of a sudden my own body felt wrong, like it didn't fit, and I pulled on a shirt.

Des noticed and grinned. "What's wrong, my man?" he whispered.

"Nothing," I said, but something *was* wrong. Those green eyes seemed like they could see right into me, past the good equipment that had led Oscar to hire me off the streets in the first place, into a secret spot where I really lived.

Lita was only in this one scene. I was the guy that was, you know, unconscious, so the doctor and his nurse—Des and Sally—came into my room, and Sally got me up. Then Des said, "Nurse, this case calls for special therapy," and he lugged a cardboard box with "RX" written on it into the room. He opened it and pulled out Lita and just sort of *put* her on me so that I kind of *wore* her. I was supposed to just barely stir, then move a little more, then more, till I was bucking like a Brahma bull. And Lita was supposed to ride me like a rodeo cowgirl, squirming and twirling, one hand in the air.

But when Des put her on, and I heard that sound—almost a sigh, "Uhhh"—my eyes popped open and I started to buck. I couldn't help myself.

My eyes locked on her face, and it closed like she was falling into herself. I wanted to say something, to explain, but I couldn't, I could only buck and breathe, feeling like she was some way pulling me into her, all of me.

"Slow down, Buddy," I heard Oscar call. "Slow down."

I couldn't. I wasn't in control. My eyes kept scanning Lita's face: it stayed closed and far away. I needed her to need me, to be with me, but I was alone. I tried to tell her and hadn't any words, only gasps. Just when I started to feel like I was gonna bawl or something, the dwarf sighed again—"Uhhh"—and her green eyes opened.

She stared directly into me and her gaze seemed to say, "I know. I understand." All the time we were still rocking. To me, it looked like she was growing, stretching out. Something was wrong: I wasn't feeling this in the right place, the only place where I'd ever felt it before. This time all of me was alight, my whole body, but more than just my body, all of me, my insides.

I heard Oscar say to somebody offstage, "Hey, this isn't bad. Would you *look* at Buddy."

It was like he was talking about someone else. I couldn't concentrate because inside me everything was moving, my lungs, my heart, my *guts*, slipping from me toward her, into her, and I heard this awful howl—"Awwwww!"— just as her eyes begun flashing like two neon signs. It wasn't her screaming, though, it was me.

I was drinking coffee alone after the scene, not wanting to have to talk to Des and Sally, not wanting to talk to anybody, even Lita, not yet anyway because I couldn't figure out what I could say, when Oscar come up behind me and patted my back. "You were great, Buddy. That was the best I ever seen you. You're going places, my boy, really going places. Am I right?"

"Thanks," I said. "Where's Lita?"

"She's gone. I paid her and she left."

"Gone? Where?" At that moment, I knew what I had to say to her.

He shrugged and relit his cigar. "Where do freaks go?" he grinned.

I sat there without saying anything for a minute. Oscar got this funny look on his face and asked, "Are you alright, kid?"

"Yeah." But I wasn't. I had to find Lita. I had to talk to her. I'd lost something, left it inside her, and I had to find her to find it. "I gotta go," I said. I was feeling real strange.

"Come on," urged Oscar, "I'll buy you kids a beer. You sure earned it today."

Matinee

Gene Autry was after this bad guy, see, and this bad guy was drivin' a car. Gene and Champ couldn't catch it, so they cut across this mountain real fast and there was lots of dust. Finally, right after Champ jumped over this fence, Gene lassoed the driver and stopped the car. That bad guy he wore a suit and tie and one of those hats like detectives wear. He had this little black mustache. Afterwards Gene Autry sang a song. I didn't like that part.

Harvey Lee Gilroy starts it, anyways. If he don't push me, I don't sock him. If I don't sock him, he don't tell his big brother and his big brother don't push me down. I'm almost at the front of the line whenever Harvey Lee starts it, and that mean ol' Mr. Banducci strolls out of the River Theater just as I sprawl on the sidewalk, so he makes *me* go clean to the very end. Not Harvey Lee or his brother, *me*. And the line is really long.

It's a ragged row of kids, that line, and it strings all the way from the picture show's box office past the jeweler's, past the men's wear shop, past the drug store, then curves with the sidewalk down El Tejon Avenue past the rear of the buildin's so that us kids at the end stand next to this great big parkin' lot.

Across it we see this big coffin of a buildin': the rear of the River Theater. I see it all the time, of course, on my way to and from school, and it always kinda shocks me to think about the connection between that ugly box and what goes on inside.

Even the picture show's front, with its colored lights flashin', its bright posters, its marquee with all those names on it, it's another world. Through those glass doors it's even better: real soft carpet, snazzy mural behind the candy counter, and the counter itself, with about a million kinds of stuff to choose from if you got the money, everything like in a technicolor movie, and smellin' the popcorn machine. On both sides of the candy counter are these red padded doors, and when you open one, you flat forget that coffin because it's like this magician just took over the dark: inside, the right things always happen.

Now all I can see is the back of the buildin' and all I can think about is that I'd be in there, oughta be if it wasn't for Harvey Lee Gilroy. Above the buildin' and parkin' lot is this faded blue sky, and below it everything's pale and dusty, not like in the movies. The line is movin' *so* slow, and all them good things are a lifetime away when you're so far around the corner that you can't even see the darn marquee, so me and Butch Renfro we jostle our way past smaller or weaker kids, then are pushed past by bigger or stronger ones, growlin' "Watch it!" low enough so they don't hear.

SCENE I, TAKE 1

"Just say I'm certain as a man can be that you can make it in college," advised Mr. Herald. "I know your friends have got jobs and cars and girls, Lloyd, but I'm asking you to take the long view."

Uncomfortable in the wooden chair, Lloyd squirmed. "I already told Mr. Findlay at the 76 station I'd be his night man," he mumbled.

"I know, Lloyd, that's why I called you to the office. I don't usually interfere like this, but you've got such potential that I wanted you to know how I feel. And I speak for the faculty too."

"Yeah, well . . ." Lloyd really didn't know what to say. Schoolwork came easy to him, true, and he was flattered that Mr. Herald had called him in and talked to him like this, but uncomfortable too. He had already mentally spent his first few checks from the gas station, and he thought he was onto an even better permanent job for summer when he finished high school. He would finish high school, at least. What did Mr. Herald want?

"I know this is hard to project, but where will you be ten years down the road? Twenty? Thirty?" asked Mr. Herald. "You've got what it takes to be someone special."

College. Nobody in his family had ever been to one. Nobody ever talked about one. That was something the fancy pants do-gooders did, go to college, something for guys who couldn't fight or get laid or get drunk, something for sissies. But he couldn't tell Mr. Herald that.

"I won't press this, Lloyd. You've got a few months before graduation. I just hope you'll continue to do good work and that you'll apply for a scholarship. You can count on my support."

Mr. Herald watched the boy slouch out of the office, one of the school's troublemakers, but different, salvageable this one, if only he could reach him.

Butch waited for Lloyd in the parking lot. "What'd ol' Herald want?"

"He was just stickin' his nose in my business."

"What'd you do?"

"I told him off."

CUT

Buster Crabbe one time I seen him grab these two big guys and shake them just like my dog does a rag. Then he let 'em drop—knocked cold—and brushed his hands off. What do ya think of that? Don't mess with ol' Buster Crabbe, boy. Another time, ol' Emperor Ming sicked about a hundred guards on Buster, but boy oh boy he really whupped 'em, sockin' and flippin' and dodgin', but not fightin' dirty, until they were all down. See what I mean?

Almost to the corner now, me and Butch extend our arms pretendin' to be fighter planes zoomin' in with machine guns, our dogfight disruptin' the line. "You be the Nip now," Butch insists.

"Naw, I'm gonna be the Flyin' Tiger again."

"You're always the Flyin' Tiger."

I can tell he's mad, so I concede, "Okay. Let's *both* be Flyin' Tigers and make them little kids be Nips." The little kids say nothing. "You guys wanna be Nips, don't ya?"

They look at one another, then nod quickly, "Uh-huh," their eyes wide.

"You always fix it so's you can be a Flyin' Tiger."

"Come on, Butch . . ."

"You always do," he insists. "You aren't fair."

"Shit!" I thrust my hands into my pockets. "This line moves too slow."

"You always do, Lloyd," Butch asserts one more time. I don't answer.

SCENE II, TAKE 1

He walked into the doghouse after another sizzling day in the oilfields, tired and ready for a beer. While he sat without a shirt airing himself before changing into street clothes, the pusher appeared in the doorway. "Lloyd, can I talk to you?"

Now what? thought the seated man. "Sure, J.D.," he said, "lemme put my shirt on." He stood and slipped it on, then strode out into the sunlight.

"Let's walk over to the pipe rack where we can talk privately," suggested the pusher.

At the rack, they squatted in the shade and J.D. got directly to the point. "I hate to tell you this, Lloyd, but John McDaniel died. He dropped dead of a stroke in his office this afternoon."

Lloyd nearly collapsed himself when he heard the message. For a long while he could say nothing. Finally, after gazing hard at the ground to control his eyes, he moaned, "Awww."

"I wish there was something I could say, but you at least know your job's safe with me," the pusher offered.

But Lloyd didn't want a safe job as a laborer, he wanted the steady promotions Mr. McDaniel had promised him when he was hired. He'd been Mr. McDaniel's boy, his favorite. The older man had been Lloyd's father's hunting partner and it had only been because of his assurances that Lloyd felt confident foregoing college. Now, squatting in the warm shade of a summer afternoon, he could see opening up before him a life of doing other people's bidding.

Later, driving home, he couldn't control his shaking hands. Why did it have to be Mr. McDaniel? Why him? Now Lloyd would go nowhere and he knew it. Everything was over for him. He swerved his pickup into the parking lot of the first bar he saw.

CUT

'Member that time John Wayne got this Nip in his sights, the same one that'd shot his buddy? What happened was that John Wayne's buddy, a good Joe, had to parachute and while he was hangin' there, this Nip let him have it. Anyways, that made John Wayne real mad, so's when he got this Nip in his sights, see, ra-ta-ta-ta-tat! The Nip was laughin' and he kinda jumped and got this real funny look on his face, then blood trickled from one corner of his mouth and his head nodded forward. His Zero started down with smoke curling back from it. Ol' John Wayne didn't smile.

I jerk Mary Kay Rutledge's pigtail, then duck as she roundhouses a punch toward me. Mary Kay nearly nails Butch, who grunts, "Hey!"

Mary Kay glares at me. "Grow up, Lloyd," she snaps.

"Sixth grader with boobs no bigger'n warts and she tells *me* to grow up," I respond, my version of a line I'd heard my big brother use.

"You dirty mouth," she spits.

Sensing eyes on me, I say, "I'll help *you* grow up, Mary Kay. Get it?" I wink at Butch.

We're on the corner in front of the drugstore, almost halfway there, and Mary Kay steps toward me. "Meaning what?" she demands.

I wink at Butch again, then raise my eyebrows like Groucho Marx. "Va-va-voom," I leer just like a guy I saw in this short.

"You're such a moron, Lloyd Pruitt!"

"I mean it, Mary Kay. You wanna go to the under-pass?"

"Save my place," she orders a girlfriend, then she's after me.

I dodge away, runnin' just fast enough to stay ahead of her, swervin' around parked cars, circlin' them with her on the other side. "Are you *that* crazy about me?" I taunt. "I really didn't know."

"You jerk, Lloyd," she screams. "You wait till I get home and tell Dale!"

Oh-oh, I'd forgotten her older brother. Now I'm in for it. I walk around her back toward the line, my stomach suddenly unsettled. Before we reach Butch and the rest, I softly call her name but she ignores me. "Honest, Mary Kay," I plead in a whisper, "I was only teasin'."

No response.

Butch grins when I slip back in line. "You really got her, boy."

"Yeah," I smile, my belly churnin'.

SCENE III, TAKE 1

"I wasn't really *with* her, Louise," he pleaded, but her eyes remained strangely cold in spite of the tears streaming down her cheeks.

"You told me, Lloyd," she choked, her chin quivering, "you told me that when we got married it was a fresh start. You said we'd both played around some before, but between us now it was for keeps."

"And it is, honey, it is."

She was having none of it. "Then you do this."

The tall man slouched across the kitchen floor and filled a glass of water at the kitchen sink to hide his confusion. What could he say? It had never occurred to him that his wife would find out or that, if she did, that she wouldn't forgive him. She always had in the past.

Before he could frame a statement, she asked, "I suppose I can start going out with men and you won't care?"

A hot coal suddenly glowed in his throat, making it impossible to swallow the water. He finally managed to croak, "I'd care."

"Then how do you think I feel? Would you forgive me if I was out sleeping with other men? Hell no! You'd probably kill me."

"No, Louise, listen. It wasn't like you think."

"Was it like I saw?"

"Honest, Louise . . ."

She cut him off: "Honest! You don't know what the word means. How many have there been, Lloyd? How many?"

"I just slipped them few times you know about, honey," he lied, desperate now.

"You promised. You promised before we were married. When we were married. After we were married. You promised and I believed you, but I never will again!"

CUT

Kissin', ugh! First ol' Elizabeth Taylor she kinda gaped at Montgomery Clift, her mouth movin' like a carp's that got thrown up on the bank. Then her eyes sorta sparkled and the picture got all fuzzy and SMACK! Us guys hooted and made loud poppin' sounds with our lips. Some girls tried to hush us, but we never until the usher flashed his light at us. Heck, I liked it better when Montgomery Clift drowned Shelley Winters. They did it again at the end, kissin' I mean, but not until Elizabeth Taylor did her carp imitation one more time. What a lousy movie.

Walkin' in slooow moootion just like the movies, meee and Buuutch. "Come on, you guys," a little kid behind us complains, "you're knockin' us outta line."

"Shut up, you little shit ass," I snap, and the kid pipes down. We go back to slooow moootion. We fake a fight, lazy leaps, deliberate ducks, sluggish socks, complete with ooofs and ooohs and a final, leisurely crumplin' to the pavement by me.

Then we're the Three Stooges, me and Butch, except there's only two of us, so we draft the little kid who complained: he gets to be the guy we do stuff to. "Oh, a wise guy, 'ey!" I challenge in Moe's voice, then bonk him on the top of his head and follow with a fake jab at his eyes.

"Nyeahhh," squeals Butch as he jerks his hand to and fro in front of the kid's face, then finishes with a final swift sweep.

I thrust my fist toward the kid and tell him to hit it. "No," he says, his chin quivering, his eyes wide and watery. "Hit it, you little . . ."

"Alright, you two!" Mr. Banducci's voice stops me. "If you two don't stop disrupting the line, you won't be allowed inside. Now straighten up." He glares at us while we look at the pavement.

Soon as he's gone, I tell Butch, "My dad can kick ol' Banducci's butt anytime."

"Mine too."

I turn toward that little kid then. "Crybaby," I hiss, then I bump him hard.

SCENE IV, TAKE 1:

Lloyd cleared his throat and rephrased the statement. "What I mean is that it ain't right them forcin' me to retire just so's they could hire some coloreds. They got no right givin' coloreds priority."

His son shrugged. "Look, Dad, what you don't see is that us whites have had priority right along. All they're trying to do is even things up to where a person's color won't make a difference. It only seems like they're getting special favors because we're used to being on top. Now that things're a little more even, it seems like we're on the bottom. It'll take time to adjust, that's all."

"Is that what they taught you in college?" asked the older man sipping from his beer. His stomach was churning as it so often did when he talked with Chad. How could his own boy have strayed so far from straight thinking?

"Let's not go through that again," his son sighed. "We've got different ways of looking at the world. I guess it just can't be helped. We're better off talking about other subjects."

But Lloyd couldn't let go. His own boy, wearing long hair and fancy clothes, living in sin with a woman up in San Francisco. His own boy, who'd never worked in fields like his daddy or worried sick over doctor's bills or had a man tell him he was through so's some colored guy could take his job, was lecturing him as usual, talking down to his own daddy. His own boy who'd even dodged the draft, humiliating him.

That was a subject beer always brought back to Lloyd, one even *he* sensed should be avoided, but that erupted like a boil once alcohol loosened him. He sat in a folding chair in front of his trailer and looked past Chad at the cottonwood trees that bordered the court. Before he could speak, his son asked, "Do you want to go fishing tomorrow? We could drive up Kern Canyon like we used to. I've got another day before I go back, so let's. What do you say?"

Lloyd was fighting not to bring up the war, his throat tight. Fishing was better than fighting, sure, but since he'd been retired, he hadn't the cash for a license or gas to drive anywhere to fish, and he didn't want to tell Chad, to poor mouth. Frustrated, he allowed the war to loom even closer to speech, grinding his teeth.

"Remember the money you loaned me when I lost my job just before I finished law school?" Chad asked.

"Yeah," croaked his father, thinking still of Vietnam, of his cowardly son.

"Well, look here." The younger man took out his wallet and withdrew five one hundred dollar bills. "We just made a killing on a judgment up in Santa Rosa and I'm clearing the slate. How much interest do I owe you?"

The war lingered, waiting to be discussed, to be argued. And Chad was probably one of those San Francisco dope smokers too. His voice tight with the effort to control himself, Lloyd managed to shake his head: "You don't owe me nothin'." You owed it to me to fight for your country against Communism, he thought but did not say.

"Hey, Dad, one thing you always taught me was to pay my debts."

Suddenly the tension within Lloyd began to break and his eyes softened. "A man's gotta help his kid the best he can. I'm just proud I's able to help," he said, shoving the war as far away as he could. "You paid me back by doin' good."

Chad reached over and grasped one of his father's lean, muscular arms and squeezed. "Hey, I just want you to know that in spite of our differences, I'm really proud you're my father. Without you, I'd never have gotten anywhere. I know your life's been rough so that mine wouldn't have to be. Let's just dwell on being family and needing each other and not fall into those old arguments, okay?" He grinned. "Okay, Daddy?"

Clearing his warm throat, Lloyd sat stiffly, blinking hard. "Let's go fishin'," he finally said.

CUT

There was Clark Gable, all old and stiff, and he was a cowboy with this real funny lady named Marilyn Monroe. They was drinkin' whiskey and chasin' horses with Eli Wallach that was a pilot and Montgomery Clift that was a rodeo rider and Thelma Ritter that was a lady herself. Ol' Marilyn Monroe didn't want Clark Gable to hurt the horses and he got real sore and finally chose her over the horses. I think Eli Wallach chose Thelma Ritter but I'm not sure. Montgomery Clift didn't get to choose anybody. Marilyn Monroe did lots of screechin' and cryin'. I guess it ended happy but nobody laughed much at the end.

The entrance at last, everybody behind me! Mr. Banducci glares as he takes my ticket and snaps it in half with one hand. "Behave yourself," he warns. I nod, hurry over the carpet to the candy counter where two ladies are standin'. They don't say nothin', but wait. Finally I say, "Good'n'Plenties." One thrusts a box toward me and takes my money.

For a second I look at the two red padded doors, then

select the left one and slip in without waitin' for Butch. I've waited too long already. Far in front of me figures flash on the screen while I creep down the aisle in what I slowly realize is a silent, almost eerie theater. My eyes finally adjust to darkness as I search for a seat, then it strikes me: it's empty. All the seats are empty and, confused, I look up at the movie.

SCENE V, TAKE 1:

"My boy's a lawyer, ya know," boasted the old man.

"Yeah," answered one of the other old timers seated on the bench, "That's what you was sayin'."

"Yessir, a lawyer."

"Well, there's too goddamn many lawyers nowadays, if you ask me," said the third grizzled man.

"Nobody asked you," snapped Lloyd. "That's what's wrong with you anyways, Turk, you're always sayin' stuff to aggravate folks."

Turk thrust his stubbled jaw forward and insisted, "Nossir, it's a fact. Too damn many of 'em. A bunch a crooked bastards."

"You callin' my boy a crook?"

"He never called your boy a crook, Lloyd," interceded Red, whose hair had long since faded to wispy, yellowish white. "Seems like I spend all my time refereein' fights between you two. Here we set with nothin' to do, waitin' on the damn undertaker, and you guys cain't but fight all the time."

"What the hell does he know about lawyers?" demanded Lloyd.

"Shit, what do any of us know? We ain't nothin' but three old buzzards that was workin' stiffs and now our workin' days are over. What do we know?" Red asked.

Lloyd responded immediately: "I know there's a hell of a lot a guy cain't learn from no school, by God. My boy's got a few things to learn himself, but at least he ain't no damn know-it-all like some, I'll say that much!"

"Smart bastard, ain't he?" Turk remarked to Red.

"You sayin' I'm dumb?"

"I'm sayin' you sound dumb, some of the things you say!"

"By God, I'll whup a man that says I'm dumb!" Lloyd eased to his feet and balled his fists.

Turk and Red remained seated. "Sit down," urged Red.

"Nossir, if you guys are gonna call me names, then you better be ready to stand up!"

"You're too damned touchy," snapped Turk.

"I coulda went to college myownself," Lloyd burst, "I was fixin' to, then *everything* fell apart and I had to go to work. Then the war, then raisin' a kid, sweatin' my ass off in the oilfields, now this, and a bunch a numb-nutted rich guys that went to college, they run everything. They run me and you and they're the ones that set us on this goddamn bench!" The old man quivered, his face more frightened than angry.

"Sit down, Lloyd," Red urged, his own expression changing, softening. "You got a point there. He's damn sure got a point, Turk. Sit on down, Lloyd."

CUT

On the screen, two old men sit on a bench arguin' with a third guy who stands in front of them. What movie is this? And where are the other kids? I turn, but Butch isn't behind me either. Where is everybody?

Suddenly one of the old men in the picture, the one standing, gasps and grabs his chest, swayin' in front of the bench, and my breath stops, my chest constricts.

"Oh," he gasps.

"Oh," I gasp.

"Oh," we gasp.

At the same instant I feel myself lifted, swept toward the screen, swooped there unable to protest, unable to resist. As the old man crumbles to the ground, I tumble into him, without breath or breadth, sucked soundlessly, arms stiff, legs immobile, colors bursting within my eyes, still bein' pulled toward some dark corner, without sight, without sound, a dismal tunnel with no light at its end.

The Great Vast-ectomy Escapade

I come in the Tejon Club that afternoon and there set the boys, all but 'cept Bob Don anyways, havin' this real serious discussion. "Shit, yeah," said Earl that run the place, "she had the biggest damn rack in our class. You shoulda seen them devils. Like mushmelons."

"Still, they wadn't no bigger'n ol' Mary Sue Rampetti's," insisted Dunc. "Yessir, she sure as hell was fun to stand in front of in the cafeteria line, them big, soft jugs a-pushin into my back. I liked to creamed my jeans ever'time she done that."

I believed him. Hell, Big Dunc used to lose his load ever'-time a gal *looked* at him, which wasn't all that often.

"She was hot for my body," added Big Dunc that had a lotta body to be hot for, most of it lard, and that was famous for not gettin' laid in high school. Half the band was diddlin' this one galfriend of his, but he was stuck playin' pocket pool.

Bob Don come in about then, draggin' his anchor a bit it looked like, and he ordered hisself a brew. I knowed he's tired because he never said nothin', no jokes even, just set there drawin' pitchers in the sweat on his beer glass while us guys kept on bullshittin'.

Wylie Hillis, this ol' retired driller that was there, he piped up, "Why is it so many gals with big tits're so damn ugly?"

That was a good question, and we all took to thinkin' about it and, after Bob Don that graduated Bakersfield Junior College and was a expert on most stuff never spoke up, I said, "Hell, that's nature's way to sorta even things out. A purty face don't *need* no big boobs."

Wylie he nodded real thoughtful.

"Just look at Dunc," I went on. "He's got that big ol' body and no plumbin' to speak of. Me, half his size, and they call me tripod."

It went clean over Dunc's head. "Huh?" he said, but the boys was laughin' to beat hell.

71

After we quieten down some, ol' Earl he asked, "Y'all remember Mary Sue's older sister, Jennie?"

"Jennie," I gasped, "you talkin' *serious* ugly now!"

That's when Bob Don finally spoke up, soundin' grouchy, "Can't you guys talk about anything but women?" he said. "That's all I ever hear around here anymore."

I started to tease him some, since he usually does his fair share of jawin' when it comes to gals, but before I could Earl responded real indignant: "Why, hell yeah! We was talkin' politics just a while back, 'member Dunc? You was saying how much you'd like to get in that lady senator's pants?"

"Damn rights!" agreed Dunc.

"What's eatin' on your liver, perfesser?" demanded Wylie that was jealous of Bob Don's education.

Bob Don he just smiled. Hearin' about politics seemed like it cheered him up some.

"Anyways," Earl went on, lookin' at me again instead of Bob Don, "I seen ol' Jennie Rampetti on the damn TV the other day just sure as hell, and she's a lawyer. A gen-u-ine law-yer! And she ain't fat no more. And she ain't ugly."

"It wadn't her," Big Dunc said flat out. "No way in hell. Ol' Jennie's prob'ly a circus fat lady nowadays."

"You never even seen the show," insisted Earl.

"Yeah, but I seen Jennie more'n once," Dunc snapped back.

"Well, mister smart-ass, I seen her and that lady that was interviewin' her she said she graduated Bakersfield High in '54, so it had to be Jennie."

"Be damned," said Dunc, a-blinkin' his eyes.

Me, I'uz semi-stunned. "I'll be go to hell," I said. "And you say she never looked too bad?"

"She looked like good nooky to me."

"And a lawyer to boot."

"Damn rights."

Nobody said nothin' for a minute, then Earl he piped up: "Any of you guys ever take ol' Mary Sue out?"

None of us had.

"Well, I did whenever we'uz seniors." His voice it sounded downright triumphant.

72

"Git anything?" asked Dunc, real anxious.

"Yeah," grinned Earl, "I got the worst case a blue balls I ever had. Looked like a damn bowlin' ball. Boy howdy was them suckers sore!"

Well, I liked to fell off my bar stool laughin' whenever ol' Earl he added, "I had to soak them suckers for a solid hour before I could to go to bed." Ever'body was hee-hawing and a-slappin' the bar, ever'body but 'cept Bob Don. That's whenever I figured somethin' was serious wrong, so I sidled next to him and asked, "What's up, pard?"

He looked at me and I could see his face was all pale. "I gotta go in the damn hospital."

"The damn hospital!" I said. "Why?"

"To get my balls carved," he said, his voice tighter'n a banjo string.

"Your balls?"

"Skeeter wants me to have a vasectomy."

"Your wife wants you to have one a them deals, how come?"

"Well," he explained, "she can't have any kids, so she says it'll make life easier on her."

"Relax," advised Earl that'd been listenin', "I had me one and it wasn't nothin'."

"Nothin' to it," Dunc agreed.

"Me, too," I told him. "I had me one. Didn't you know that? Right after our fourth was born. Course in my case, they called it a vast-ectomy."

Even Bob Don laughed. Then he said, "I just don't like the idea of someone cutting that area."

"Hey, that's a disaster area anyways," I said, and ever'-body laughed again.

"Nothin' to it," Big Dunc repeated.

"Me, I don't cotton to doctors none," Wylie Hillis told us. "Back in Arkansas where I come from don't nobody go to one. Don't need to."

"Bullshit," said Dunc that don't exactly admire Wylie.

About then ol' Shoat Whilhite that don't belong to Big Dunc's fan club mosied in and give us a howdy. I filled him in on Bob Don's vast-ectomy. Things was quiet for a minute, what with so many don't-likes sittin' together and all, then Earl he volunteered, "Hell, I'll save you the money and do 'er myself, just as a favor. I got my fishin' knife out in the pickup. Wait a minute and I'll go fetch that sucker."

"Fat chance," exhaled Bob Don. "I've seen you clean fish."

"Ain't no fish ever complained."

"That's because they all died," added Shoat, and we laughed again.

Wylie took his old straw cowboy hat off and scratched his spotted dome. "What the hell is a *vast-ectomy* anyways?"

"You ever castrate a calf?" asked Dunc.

Bob Don give him a sour look.

"Don't be a chicken-shit," Dunc sneered.

It looked like to me Bob Don was gettin' semi-tired of Dunc's big mouth, but he'd have no chance if he took a swing at that big sucker, so I said to Wylie, a-hopin' to break the tension, "It's whenever the doc he cuts them little tubes in your sack so's you can't make no more babies."

"He cuts on you *there*?"

"Nothin' to it," said Dunc. "You ain't got nothin' to lose anyways."

"Not me," Wylie puffed. "Nosir, not this ol' boy."

"It really ain't all that bad," said Shoat.

Wylie said he wondered did it hurt, and I said naw, but I'uz sore for a week or so after.

"Nothin' to it," advised Dunc.

"All you guys had it done?" asked Bob Don, soundin' relieved.

Me and Earl and Shoat all nodded. Wylie he put his hand on his fly like he's protectin' somethin'. Dunc said, "Nothin' to it."

Finally, Bob Don he said, "When did you have it done, Dunc?"

"Me? Are you shittin'? I ain't lettin' no sawbones carve on my gear!"

"Hell," I said, "they couldn't find no tools small enough to work on Dunc anyways."

"Your ass," he grunted, givin' me a hard look.

"That's because in his case there's nothin' to it," added Shoat, and Dunc he come off his bar stool with his fists balled.

Shoat, that'd fight a damn gorilla, he hopped right down and went nose-to-nose with the big guy, and us boys we right away separated 'em. Besides, Dunc never looked too anxious to tangle with a guy that'd swarmed him a few years back, so it didn't take much tuggin' to pull him away. He was bluffin', I believe.

That broke up the party. Dunc took off and so did Shoat. D'rectly, Wylie Hillis did too, still a-clutchin' his fly like he'd been wounded. Me, I walked out into the parkin' lot with Bob Don that looked like he's a-feelin' better. "It really ain't that much," I assured him.

"Yeah, I guess," he grinned, 'but I've never had any surgery anywhere, let alone *there*, so I'm a little wary."

"Hey," I admitted, "I'uz scared shitless, but it wasn't bad. And Heddy she felt a lot better about things afterwards, if you know what I mean. It 'uz a good move for me."

"Thanks," he said, "that makes me feel better."

"When're you havin' it done?"

"Next week."

"Just hang loose," I advised. "Drink a few medicinal spirits in here at Dr. Earl's and you'll be fine."

"Good enough," he grinned, then climbed into his pickup and started its engine. Just then who should swing back into the parkin' lot but Big Dunc. He come outta his truck and swaggered over to us like we'uz gonna have a shootout, but when he got next to us he said, "That damn Shoat better watch it or I'll have to kick his ass."

"Yeah," I said real dry.

"And besides, Bob Don," he added, "I been to one a them vast-ectomy oriental sessions myownself, that's why I know there ain't nothin' to it."

"Oriental?" I puzzled.

"Orientation," Bob Don corrected.

"Same difference," snorted Big Dunc.

"Hey!" Bob Don added real quick, "if you've been to the orientation, why haven't you had one?"

"You callin' me chickenshit?" snapped the big man.

"I'm asking why."

I chimed in: "Yeah, Dunc, why?"

"Listen here, Bob Don, I'll tell you this much: if a little peckerhead like you gets one, I *sure* as hell will. I'll march down there the minute you get yours."

"Guaranteed?" I said.

"You callin' me a liar?"

Ol Dunc'uz really on edge, so I just said, "Nope. But we'll be checkin' with ya."

That whole next week, Dunc kept carryin' on in front of ever'body, insistin' there wasn't nothin' to it. Between him and that damned ol' Wylie Hillis howlin' about how doctors just screw folks up, well they about undid all the good I'd done reassurin' ol' Bob Don. He got tenser and tenser as the big day come closer, and Dunc for some reason kept on runnin' his mouth.

"Yessir," Dunc he told this one drummer that come in, "take a look at Bob Don there. He's about to get nutted." Another time, Dunc called out whenever this colored singer with a real high voice come on a TV show, "He sounds just like Bob Don's a-gonna." About the only time he shut up was when ol' Shoat come in; I guess Dunc never wanted to have to kick his ass.

Anyways, I could tell how much he was a-gettin' under Bob Don's skin, so I finally called him on it. "Why don't you just butt out, Dunc?" I challenged.

"Maybe you want your little ass whupped," he snapped right back.

"Let's go!"

Before the big turd could roll off his bar stool, Earl spoke up: "You start any shit, Duncan, and you'll never drink another beer in this place. So either shut your fuckin' trap or find another place to hang out." Earl sounded hot and Dunc knew he meant what he said, so he cooled it. He also knew Earl kept a sawed-off pool cue and a shotgun under the bar. Besides, Dunc never had no other friends, so we had him by the short hairs. He finished his beer, then said, "I'll come back whenever you guys ain't so touchy," and left.

And that's when I come up with the scheme. "Listen," I said, "it's time we shut that big prick up. He said he'd go in and have a vasectomy if you did, right?"

"Right," agreed Bob Don.

"Okay, and you're a-goin' in on Friday, right?"

"Right."

"Then on Thursday we give Mr. Duncan a little taste of his own medicine."

What made it double-good was that Thursday was Big Dunc's day off, so whenever I got off work that afternoon and hit the club, he'd been there a long time pourin' beer down his neck. I slipped onto the stool next to him, and said, "Well, I wonder how Bob Don's a-doin' over at the hospital?"

"This the day?" snorted Dunc, that had his nose semi-outta-joint ever since I stood up to him.

"Yep. Fact is, it's prob'ly all done by now. He said he might drop by to have a beer on his way home."

"I cain't wait to hear him talk," said Dunc tryin' to sound smart, but soundin' nervous instead.

Just then in stumbled ol' Wylie Hillis. "Where's the per-fesser?" he asked right away.

"Gettin' hisself nutted," answered Dunc real smart alecky.

I let it slide and Earl, that knew about the plan, he winked at me. I ordered another beer and listened to the juke box and waited. D'rectly, just like we planned, up drove Bob Don. Dunc he heard the diesel pickup and said, "That must be him." He never sounded too chipper. I guess he'uz remem-berin' his promise.

After a minute, the front door it swung open, and in hob-bled Bob Don on these crutches we'd borrowed, lookin' like the ass end of bad luck. He moaned real loud each step he took, and made a face. "Damn," said Dunc.

"I may not have no education," said Wylie Hillis, a-headin' for the door, lookin' like he could lose his beer any sec-ond, "but I'm too damn smart to let any sawbones cut on me." Out he went.

I swung down from my stool and helped Bob Don get settled next to Dunc. Immediately—I mean *right now*—Dunc come off his seat and said, "Well, reckon I gotta ramble."

"Wait up," I said. "When're you a-goin' in for your operation, Dunc?"

"I got errands to run for the ol' lady," he said.

"Bob Don's did it," I pointed out, "now it's your turn."

"I'll get around to it," he spit, soundin' semi-pissed and more than semi-scared.

"How was it, Bob Don?" asked Earl, and I could tell that Dunc wanted to hear and never wanted to at the same time. He sorta hovered there right behind where Bob Don set.

"Oh," said Bob Don real weak, "it was rough."

"I'll bet," Earl nodded.

"Well, that vast-ectomy cain't be too bad if you guys all had one. It can't be too rough a-tall," Dunc said, a little of that fake courage a-creepin' back into his voice. "Don't make such a big deal out of it."

Seein' that Bob Don had survived, Dunc was gettin' flat brave. He climbed back onto his stool to finish the half-a-glass a beer he'd left. "I might just go and get me one d'rectly. Nothin' to it, anyways."

"Naw," Bob Don agreed, "nothin' to it. And they even let me keep these." He reached into his pocket and pulled out the damn *piece a resistance*, them bloody sheep testicles we'd picked up at Pascal Ansolobehere's ranch that mornin', and he held 'em out to Big Dunc.

Dunc timbered, a-keelin' over stool and all, hollerin' "*Ho-ly shit!* Get them thangs away from me! Get them nasty thangs away!" His face looked like a cue ball. He scuttled toward the door with Bob Don after him, a-holdin' them sheep nuts out and sayin', "Come on, Dunc. There's nothing to it. Let's call the doctor right now."

"No way, you crazy bastard," cried the big guy as he scrambled out the door, "no way in hell!" Dunc jumped in his truck and spun rubber clean up to Chester Avenue a-makin' his getaway. The last thing we seen was two giant eyes a-starin' at us as he fishtailed away.

Bob Don he turned back toward me and Earl, still holdin' them balls in one hand, a big grin on his face. "Well," he said, "let's talk politics. What was that lady senator's name?"

Crossing the Valley

My grandfather's blotched hand quivered to his temple and brushed; he leaned squeakily back in his smooth wooden chair, his high-top shoes leaving the floor, then he swung forward until they were flat and firm again. Finally he spoke: "We used to take a big wagon from here across the central valley into the hills and up to Yosemite, my folks and Jasper and me." He rustled about his heaped desk— "I've got a picture here somewhere"—and he glanced at the withered corkboard above the desk's rolltop to see if the photo he sought was pinned there, but couldn't find it among the brittle notes and browning photos and business cards of long-dead wholesalers.

For a moment his eyes caught and held the picture of a fierce young man in a football uniform. He pointed his not-quite-straight finger at the fading photo of his son—my father—"That's my boy," he said, pausing, staring into and over a gulf of lost years.

"I recollect," he continued, momentarily sounding like a man who had recently wept, "I recollect as how my folks and Jasper and me would cross into the valley over the pass up by Paso Robles and come out right near Coalinga. Hotter'n hell it was. And we'd go straight across as we could, but we'd always have to camp in that damned hot valley. The horses hated it as much as we did." He chuckled privately, his yellow sparse teeth exposed. For another moment he mouthed silent words, then he was standing.

"I better go sweep-up," he announced, already shuffling stooped out of his small office toward the closet where he stored his janitorial equipment. He had never paid a custodian to clean his store, doing the work himself after his sons had grown. He left me alone sitting next to his scarred desk while he pushed green sawdust over the floor of the store, much to the obvious embarrassment of my Aunt Lenore who was waiting on a customer at the time.

Grandpa was eighty-years-old then and, as Aunt Lenore put it, failing. Yet he walked half-a-mile to the store every morning at six and swept it thoroughly; then he'd move out front and sweep the sidewalk. After finishing his custodial tasks, he'd walk to the businessmen's coffee shop in the lobby of the Hart House—both of which he owned— and have breakfast.

Late afternoons he swept the store once again, customers mincing steps to avoid his determined broom thrusts. He moved as inexorably as a creeping glacier, and at about the same pace, toward the front of the store. It was usually near closing time when he finished.

The town had long since outgrown him and the store. Stylish shops now surrounded his unchanging dry-goods emporium that had years ago exchanged goods for farm produce. Now the store lost money, selling only to old families and to the diminishing numbers who earned their livings on the soil, mostly Mexicans and Filipinos, as well as a small group of young people from a nearby commune; everyone bought on credit with 1910 interest rates. "We just don't attract your better-class patrons," Aunt Lenore had once explained to me, which meant that none of her country-club friends needed steel-toed boots or sunbonnets. Grandpa sold working people's clothes: overalls, denim shirts, gloves, no-nonsense print dresses and, if you looked closely, you could still find celluloid collars in one aging glass case. His other holdings—the hotel and the houses and farms and office buildings, and the stocks and bonds—easily absorbed the store's small losses.

Now his family, all except my father, had decided to liquidate the store and retire Grandpa, but in order to do so they had to have him declared incompetent. I was in town to join my father at a family counsel and unofficial business meeting to be held that evening.

Grandpa eventually shuffled back into his office, stopping abruptly at the door when he saw me sitting near his desk. "Yes?" he said, gazing hard from behind his faded blue, nearly colorless, eyes.

"It's me, Grandpa," I replied. "Bud, your grandson."

"Bud?"

"Frank's boy."

His gaze softened, then he moved to the old wooden swivel chair and plopped stiffly into it. "When we got to Yosemite we'd pitch our tent on a meadow next to the river. Jesus that was a pretty place. Jasper—do you know my brother Jasper?—Jasper and me used to swim in that cold booger, and catch big trout. Hell of a place." He reached into the upper drawer of his desk and withdrew a lint-covered twist of chewing tobacco and held it tentatively in his thin, veined hand as though weighing it. "I haven't seen Jasper today, have you?"

"No." Jasper died before I was born.

"Haven't seen 'im, huh? Well . . .," he stood and shuffled toward the door, thrusting the tobacco plug into his vest pocket, "let's go get us a glass of beer."

I followed him out the back door into the softening glare of a late afternoon, walking up the unpaved alley into a door at the rear of an old billiard parlor.

As we sipped cold beer to the muted, sensual clicks of snooker balls, to the voices and laughter of working men relaxing to the twang of country music from a juke box, Grandpa reminisced. "Used to be a big mirror right up there," he said pointing behind the bar. "Old Charley Johnston claimed it was the biggest in the world. And a brass rail. It ran the whole length of this place back to where the pool tables are now. Used to be quite a saloon. Prohibition changed all that. Old Charley died and his kid took over and made this a pool hall. Good old Charley."

An argument broke out at one of the rear tables and, amid much pushing and cursing, two young men surrounded by a clutch of interested parties, strode out to an alley to settle their differences. The few old-timers at the bar chuckled, but stayed with their beers. "Looks like a little beef," Grandpa said. "One time me and Jasper got in a fight with the Gomez boys, Paco and Trini, in here. That was a hell of a fight. It was over their sister Lupe, my special gal." He drifted away for a moment. Lupe Gomez had eventually become his wife, my grandmother. She died

81

when my father was a small boy, during the great flu epidemic of 1918.

"Who won?" I asked.

He chuckled, "Those Gomez boys kicked hell out of us." A long pause. "God but she was a woman," he said, his faded eyes softening, syrupy tears welling. In a moment his sunken cheeks glistened.

"Let's go," I said, pushing gently at his elbow. We walked out the front door and around the block to my car, then drove to the old family home where Grandpa lived with Aunt Lenore and her brood. The clan was gathering there.

It was some meeting. Everyone came with their minds made up as near as I could tell, and emotion prevailed over reason. Grandpa, who wasn't present, by the way, was through and that was that. Aunt Lenore read a report that proved, she claimed, the store was a losing venture. "And besides," she said gravely, "Poppa's tired. He's earned a rest." He's earned the right to decide for himself, I suggested, but she ignored me.

My father fought the rest of the family, giving them no quarter, conceding them nothing. He countered Lenore by reading the last annual report figures showing that the family corporation was overwhelmingly in the black. "So what if we lose a few dollars to keep Pop happy? Where would any of *you* be without him?" Uncle Willard whined a reply, and Aunt Lenore mouthed silent words, but father cut them off. "If you retire him to death," he said with sudden venom, his eyes glowing, "I'll make every one of you sorry you were ever born." He glared at them and they looked at their feet and twisted their white, soft hands.

Still, when it came to a vote, my various uncles and my aunt all voted to retire Grandpa. Lenore was authorized to develop a more profitable plan for the building. "We'll see," father said as we left the meeting, his jaw muscles flexing. Uncle Kent tried to shake father's hand when we passed him, but father told him to shake hands with Lenore.

Six months later Uncle Willard and his wife Kay brought Grandpa to share a spaghetti dinner with my wife,

Carmen, our twins, and me. He was "theirs" for the month, as Kay put it.

Grandpa was a different man. He shuffled uncertainly and depended on a cane, an obscene parody of the wiry cuss who had walked to and from work, who had scattered able-bodied men with his determined broom strokes. And he rarely spoke, not seeming to know or care where he was or if he was.

Father had been right. After a couple of stiff Scotch and sodas, Uncle Willard finally admitted as much. "Bud," his voice was warm, though I thought I detected a kernel of fear, "you've got to talk to your father. He's got things all wrong. He'll think Poppa's condition has been caused by his retirement. Doctor Peely says it probably would have happened anyway. You've got to reason with your father."

"That's between you two," I answered.

"No, you don't know him . . ."

I gave him an incredulous look, and his tone changed. "No, you really don't, I mean it. He's a cold man, your father, and he's vindictive. He makes his mind up and that's it. When he was a kid there wasn't anyone around who'd stand up to him in a fight. He's vicious."

There was, I could see, truth in what Willard said, but he exaggerated. Willard was basically a good guy, and I found myself a little sorry for him, but when I noticed Grandpa staring blankly at the playpen in which his great-grandchildren frolicked, I went cold. "You knew that," I said, taking Willard's glass and Grandpa's into the kitchen where the women cooked.

When I returned with fresh drinks Grandpa had picked up my twin son, and held him snugly against his chest. "Poppa, you shouldn't," Uncle Willard was saying, moving toward Grandpa.

"Leave him alone," I ordered, more harshly than I intended, adding, "He's okay."

We finished our drinks and I was beginning to feel a slight buzz. Willard loosened-up too. "Your father hasn't got any right to criticize us," he told me. "He could've joined the family business—God knows Poppa wanted him to—but he didn't. We stayed and we're all stuck in San Luis till we die.

He's a big shot over there in the valley, but he still criticizes us. It's not fair."

Feeling sorry for himself, I thought, jealous of Father's independence. A couple of more drinks and Willard will reveal all the family's secrets. I felt a little like giggling, but only nodded and mumbled, "Uhmmm."

"It's really not fair. And you know what's worse? Poppa always favored your father. He really did." He took a long pull from his glass. "It's because he was a football star. That's how he won his scholarship to college, and that's how he made all those business contacts. That *damned* football!" He nearly knocked his drink over as he gestured emphatically.

Just as I was framing a reply, Grandpa, who was seated across the room and who both of us had really forgotten as our soggy conversation continued, began chuckling loudly. "Football?" he said. "By God, my boy Frank can play football. He's a rough customer, Frank."

He chuckled again, and Uncle Willard gave me an exasperated shrug. "When I was a kid I played on the town team," Grandpa went on. "Back in those days we didn't wear fancy uniforms, just work clothes with ribbons tied on our arms so you could tell who was on your side. We played Taft one time—or was it Santa Maria—no, Atascadero it was, and these two big fellas on our team, Turk Jordon and Red Sousa, they just picked me up and threw me clear over the scrum, and the goal too, for a touchdown.!" He nodded, winked, then laughed the way a man does when he pokes you in the ribs.

Finally dinner was served. Carmen, my wife, always liked Grandpa and gave him special attention, keeping his plate and wineglass full. Perhaps it was the liquor I'd consumed, but dinner was nearly finished before I noticed that Grandpa was calling Carmen "Lupe." Willard was too far gone to notice, but his wife raised an eyebrow and flashed me a knowing smirk. Carmen, of course, had ignored the name change. Just as she was serving coffee, Grandpa gave her an affectionate pat on her bottom. Willard's wife gasped.

and Uncle Willard, once he realized what had happened, began apologizing sloppily. I told him to forget it and Carmen just smiled.

Two months later Grandpa fell and broke his hip; a day later he suffered a stroke while in the hospital. After my father telephoned me—"Pop's about had it," he said. "You'd better hurry."—I rushed to San Luis Obispo.

It was too late for normal visiting hours when I reached the hospital, but Grandpa's physician was an old friend of Father's so he let my dad and me into the room where Grandpa lay comatose, a putty imitation of himself. With tubes running in and out of him, he resembled nothing so much as a bulky splice in the smooth hoses.

I stood with Father next to the bed, feeling more fatigued than involved at that moment. I was about to nudge my dad to go, when Grandpa's head twitched a bit and he seemed to sigh. His head rolled so that he faced us. For a moment we looked at him, then we turned to leave. Just as we reached the door, something grabbed me, something inside I mean, and I glanced back at Grandpa one more time. His eyes were flickering off and on like reluctant fluorescent lamps—his beautiful old eyes—and I felt Father stiffen beside me. Grandpa's eyes met mine right away and without confusion stared at me for a long moment. Then, as though finishing a conversation, he spoke: "Crossing that hot valley was rough," he said weakly, yet clearly, "rougher'n hell. But it was worth it to get to them mountains. God what a place."

His eyes blinked momentarily, appearing to fade, then flashed back on, staring at Father. "Frank," he whispered, "your momma's dead. It wasn't your fault, boy, it was the damn flu. We couldn't do anything." His voice faded a bit as he continued, "We couldn't do a damn thing." One of his hands fluttered toward Father, who grasped it—the only outward sign of affection I can ever remember having seen pass between them. Father had tears about to break over the rim of his eyes and his mouth was a sudden slash. "We tried, but we couldn't do a damn thing," Grandpa gasped, his faded eyes losing focus, wandering.

Father put Grandpa's hand back on the bed. "Lupe?" Grandpa said, his eyes beginning to glaze. "Lupe?" he said once more just as his gaze went blank. We thought he was dead, but he lived two more days. After the funeral, Father and Carmen and I drove home, over the hills back into the valley.

Vengeance

They filled the tiny stucco porch with their bodies and their voices, a thick boy carrying several bicycle tires looped like thick black bracelets over one grimy arm, and a smaller boy shoeless but wearing a tattered shirt. "You better git off my daddy's property, Bertil, or I'm callin' the sher'ff!" shouted the larger of the two. He shook a fleshy fist in the other's face, but the pale, slight boy did not budge.

"Whan I aim a do is git na evinence own nyou, Namar!" the smaller boy yelled back, his narrow arms tight at his sides, his thin fists white. A large, white hearing-aid protruded from one of his ears, and a slim wire extended from it along his neck into the bulging breast pocket of his shirt.

"What the hell's that noise?" roared a voice from within the house.

"It's this dummy, Daddy," called Lamar, then he grinned tightly at the smaller boy: "Now you gonna git it, dummy."

"Whan I aim a do . . .," the smaller boy was repeating when a vast man lurched through the screen door onto the porch, forcing the debaters onto the small bare space that constituted a yard. Like the heavy boy, the man wore a dirty t-shirt without sleeves; and his thick arms were rippled with fat that stretched his fading tattoos into textured frescoes. Perched jauntily on the side of a head that might have been a pale pumpkin was a greasy baseball cap, and a toothpick extended from the man's mouth like a serpent's single fang. Nearly hidden in the span of one vast hand was a can of beer. "What're you doin' here, boy?" he demanded, his eyes creased with threat.

"Namar snole my nike, Misner Snudly, an I aim a git na evinence own him," the thin boy insisted.

"Lamar never stole nothin'," Mr. Studly asserted, wiggling his toothpick. "Now git your ass off this property before I let Lamar whup you."

"Whan I aim a do . . ."

"Git!" exploded the man, and Bertil scrambled through stacks of old automobile tires until he stood on the dirt border between yard and street, where he planted himself, shook one small fist and yelled: "Whan I aim a do is git na evinence own nyou, Namar!" then he turned and walked awkwardly away, arms and legs not quite synchronized.

The man on the porch shook his large head. "Ain't that kid a sorry specimen," he observed, tugging at his jeans so that they hung briefly on the impossible angle of his belly before slipping back to their customary camp below the slope. "What's wrong with him?"

"He's just a dummy is all, in the re-tard class at school, and he's about deaf. He can't even talk right," Lamar explained with a chuckle.

He was still chuckling when his father smacked his face with an open hand. "How's come you to steal that boy's bike?" the man demanded.

The fat boy cringed. "I never," he insisted.

"Don't shit me. I know you never *found* all them bikes I seen you tote through here."

Backing away several steps, the boy asked, "Where'd *you* git all them tires?"

The small, stucco house was an oasis in a black rubber badland, a wilderness of vulcanized pinnacles and peaks, of retreaded dunes and drifts; tentative tracks extended into that rubber wasteland, disappeared into canyons and draws where secret sheds and gleaming piles of hubcaps hid. At the end of one trail, the body of an ancient Chevy lay rusting, its engine suspended from an A-frame like a forgotten sacrifice. The core of the paths was not the house, but a large aluminum building in which Lamar's father mysteriously converted threadbare tires into thickly-treaded reincarnations to be shipped far out-of-state, where their rubber would strip faster than song-leaders at drive-in movies.

Mr. Studly grinned like a clever jack-o-lantern. "Well, I never stole none of 'em *myself*. I cain't say how my suppliers got 'em." The man lifted one thick leg and farted thunderously—"Ooops, stepped on a frog"—he winked at his son and reentered the small house.

As soon as his father disappeared, Lamar shuffled quickly along a path to the small shed in which he secreted his inventory of bikes. Inside, he snapped on the bare bulb, then from under a wooden bench he extracted a warm can of beer stolen from his father's supply in the pantry, and a girlie magazine from his own collection. He took a long pull from the can, and sneezed, warm bubbles having invaded his nose. "Shit!" he said.

At fourteen-and-a-half, Lamar Studly remained in the sixth grade and counted the days until his sixteenth birthday when he could legally quit school. He didn't mind remaining a sixth grader again, because his bulk allowed him to bully his classmates. Among them he was known as a tough customer. Fortunately, most boys his own age or older also treated him deferentially in the hope they might be awarded an occasional tire or hubcap, or perhaps a glimpse at his famous magazine collection, so he moved with blessed impunity through Oildale's streets, little hindered by parental restriction or peer pressure.

Moreover, Lamar had stumbled upon a business when a Mexican man who supplied tires to his father had one day asked the boy if he might be able to provide used bicycles for resale in Los Angeles. Lamar had been doing just that unbeknownst to all in Oildale until that fateful day when Bertil had spied him slipping away from the River Theater on the dummy's broken-down Flyer, which had hardly been worth stealing as it turned out. Well, if there was one thing Lamar could handle, it was a dummy. Except this one refused to be handled.

In fact, Bertil had confronted Lamar after school that very next Monday, and right in front of the guys. "I sneen nya Namar! I wont my nike!"

"I ain't got your shitty bike, dummy, now git outta here."

"I sneen nya!"

"You see about as good as you hear," Lamar had said,

and the guys all laughed.

"Whan I aim a do is git na evinence own nyou, Namar."

"You better not bother me no more or I'll kick your ass," the large boy had warned, a threat that would have ended matters if a sensible kid had been involved.

Bertil lived in a raw wooden hovel near the Kern River, one of nearly a dozen children in a family that seemed desperately poor even in that unprosperous area. Like all his brothers and sisters, his skin appeared perpetually covered by a dirt patina, a mysterious darkness that led some to speculate that they were gypsies, others to suggest that the small house into which the family crowded contained no bath. His hair was permanently burred in a home haircut, and he wore shoes only to school; socks were added for church.

Six mornings a week, shortly after dawn, Bertil's parents, along with several of his older siblings, piled in an ancient truck and drove away, only to return after dark. They were said to be "pickers," a word spoken in hushed, almost frightened tones by townsfolks like a dark incantation from their shared past. After school, while other younger children could be seen grazing their lawnless yard—it was considered little short of miraculous in the neighborhood the way those kids stayed home—Bertil delivered *The Bakersfield Californian.*

The boy had for several months covered his newspaper route on foot until he had saved enough money from the small part of his earnings that he kept for himself to purchase an old bicycle at the police auction in Bakersfield. Only a month later, he had spied Lamar Studly pedaling away on it. Although he had told his teacher, and Lamar had been called into the principal's office, nothing had been proven since—as the fat boy knew but did not admit—the wayward bike had already been trucked to Southern California. It had not been a rigorous inquiry in any case, because the claims of students in the Special Class seldom amounted to much; when Lamar's father, a locally respected businessman, had sworn that his son was innocent, the investigation had been terminated. Mr. Studly had dutifully slapped Lamar a couple of times for the real crime of almost allowing himself to be caught, then forgot the matter. Or forgot it until that afternoon when Bertil showed up on their porch.

Sitting in his shed, Lamar sipped warm beer and pondered this new turn of events, the dummy confronting him here, at his own house. Bertil wasn't going to be calling the cops; it was too late for that. Still, some of Lamar's friends were kidding him about bicycles, sometimes in front of other people, and that dumb kid was staring at him all the time at school, and accusing him when he got the chance. A few teachers were now eyeing Lamar closely too. The fat boy considered his options. He could beat the kid up, but some big kid would take up for the dummy sure as anything, and then he would really be in for it. He could lay low for awhile, let his business go, but then he wouldn't have the money he needed to keep his pals happy. Lamar sighed: it wasn't fair.

When the fat boy entered the house that evening for dinner, his father grabbed him by the shirt and growled, "I don't want that little turd comin' back here no more, understand?"

"Okay, Daddy."

"And I ain't shittin'."

Mr. Studly's eyes looked like yellow lifesavers and his son suspected that his old man had worked his way through his daily case of beer thinking about that dummy. He also knew that the man was quick to throw punches when drunk, so he decided to say as little as possible. "Okay, Daddy."

"Now go eat," the man grunted, releasing his son. "And go easy. You're gittin' too fat."

"Okay, Daddy."

That next day at school during recess, Lamar and two of his cronies were sneaking cigarettes behind the gym when they noticed Bertil standing across the playfield staring at them. "Looky," observed Talcott, "that dummy's lookin' at ya again."

"Whyn't you just kick his ass?" Buzzard asked.

"Hey, Buzz, I might have to, but I don't wanna hurt the re-tard." Lamar was carefully combing a greasy black curl onto his forehead. He returned his comb to a pocket.

"Here he comes," Talcott said.

Lamar looked up and saw that, sure enough, Bertil was walking straight toward him, and he felt his stomach suddenly churn. Damn him, Lamar thought. Well maybe I *will* just kick his ass. But when the thin boy stood directly in front of him, Lamar felt vaguely sick.

"I aim a git na evinence own nyou, Namar," Bertil said, his beady eyes looking straight into the fat boy's. Somethin' strange about them eyes, too, Lamar thought, somethin' real strange: they never had no depth; they just seemed to be ... well ... *there*. He didn't even like the dummy looking at him. Belly burning, Lamar said nothing, but he felt as though he was being inflated, pumped full of air so that his skin grew tighter and tighter, while Bertil continued talking.

"I sneen you sneal my nike an' I aim a git na evinence."

For one final instant, Lamar quivered, so full that his skin felt ready to burst, then he snorted—"Nooo!"—and threw a wild, roundhouse punch that smacked the smaller boy to the ground and shattered his large white hearing aid.

"Good punch, Lamar!" exalted Buzzard, jumping in his excitement.

Talcott's voice was less pleasant: "Yeah, but you broke his hearin' aid. I'm gittin' outta here. You're in Dutch now, Lamar."

The fat boy, feeling suddenly free and triumphant, was shuffling a quick circle around Bertil, who held his bleeding ear with both hands and wept quietly, shattered white plastic scattered in front of him like bits of bone. "Come on," taunted Lamar, "you want some more?" His fists were poised.

"What's going on here?" demanded the gym teacher who had just rounded the corner.

Dropping his hands immediately, Lamar gulped, "Uh ... this kid fell down."

He was expelled from school, and his father had to buy Bertil a new hearing aid as well as pay all medical expenses. On top of that, in order to avoid a lawsuit, Mr. Studly had to settle a sum of money on Bertil's parents. It was the worst time of Lamar's life, and it was all the dummy's fault.

Lamar didn't mind not attending school, but he did mind the daily slaps and punches, the constant nagging, and he resented being restricted to his own yard, a penalty that caused his bicycle business to fall apart. Most of all, he minded Bertil, who each afternoon while wandering his newspaper route, planted himself for several minutes in front of the Studly property and stared. After shouting threats at the boy and making every obscene gesture he could remember, Lamar had become frustrated and, in fact, had begun hiding within the house and peeping through drawn curtains at the appointed hour. It was all so crazy: he could kick that kid's ass, yet *he* was hiding.

Nearly a month after the incident at school, the frustrated fat boy determined to escape his confinement in the hubcap hills and whitewall canyons no matter what the consequences. Despite his supply of warm beer and girlie magazines, he felt the need for comradeship. A quick jaunt down to the Tejon Club for a game of eight-ball with his chums was what he needed. Besides, Mr. Studly was gone that afternoon delivering tires, so escape would be no problem.

After traveling sidestreets and alleys, Lamar slipped in the back door of the pool hall; he didn't want any of his father's cronies seeing him. Once inside, though, caution left him, and he called, "Hey Buzz! Hey Talcott!" His pals appeared surprised, then delighted: "Hey Lamar! Hey big guy!" They patted his back and he bought them cokes. While they shot pool, the three boys laughed their way through versions of the fateful fight: "You really duked that re-tard, Lamar," chuckled Buzzard, who had himself been briefly suspended from school. "He's lucky that teacher come," added Talcott, who had avoided penalty. "That dummy'll never mess with you no more."

"He *better* not," warned Lamar, feeling easy. Talcott slapped his back.

The Tejon Club's front door opened and a small figure entered wearing a newspaper bike bag over his shoulders like a serape. He handed the bartender a copy of the *The Californian*, then turned to leave when Buzzard noticed him; "Hey, it's the dummy. Look, it's the dummy. Let's git him."

"Wait a minute," Lamar said.

"Yeah, come on," urged Talcott.

"No, wait," the fat boy insisted.

Bertil was at the door when he glanced back and saw the trio. He turned and walked directly to Lamar. "Whan I aim a do, Namar, is git na evinence own nyou," he said.

"Hit him, Lamar," called Talcott.

"Kick his butt," Buzzard exhorted.

"Git away from me," the fat boy threatened, but Bertil did not move.

"Whan I aim a do . . ."

"Git, damnit!" Lamar shouted and he pushed the smaller boy, who stumbled to the floor.

The bartender and two customers who had been sipping beer at the counter hurried to the fallen boy. "What's goin' on here?" demanded the large man wiping his hands on a bar towel.

"This kid called me a name," said Lamar.

The two customers helped Bertil up, while the bartender growled at the fat boy: "Maybe you oughta pick on someone your own size."

"That kid better quit callin' me names," Lamar countered.

"He snole my nike," Bertil said.

"I never."

"Oh," said the bartender, his voice even more ominous, "is this the bully that beat up on you?"

The small boy nodded.

"You three better get outta here," ordered the glowering man, his hands kneading the bar towel. "I don't want you back ever. Do you understand?" His eyes were blazing and his voice had become strangely soft. "Ever."

Lamar said nothing. Buzzard and Talcott were already scuttling toward the backdoor.

"One more thing," the bartender added. "Don't let me hear about you so much as touchin' this boy again or I'll kick your ass so far up your back you'll have to take your hat off to shit, get me?"

"Yeah," Lamar croaked.

"I aim a git na evinence own nyou, Namar," Bertil said as the fat boy turned to leave, and Lamar felt like putting his fingers in his ears.

That night, Mr. Studly raged into his son's room. "Bob down at the Tejon Club called and said you was in there causin' trouble today after I told you not to leave the yard. He said you was pickin' on that deaf kid again. You just cain't leave him alone, can you? Well maybe this'll learn you," he hissed as he began swinging at his son.

Locked in his room the next afternoon, Lamar peered with horrid fascination through drawn curtains at Bertil who was standing and staring at the house from outside the yard, his newspaper bag suspended from his shoulders, his new hearing aid protruding like a wen. He's not just dumb, Lamar concluded, he's nuttier than a fruitcake is what he is. The fat boy felt like crawling under the bed to avoid those hot, beady eyes, but it seemed to him that they would find him no matter where he hid. After Bertil finally departed, Lamar scurried out the window and hustled through foothills of bias plies and belted plies, arroyos of snow treads and tractor treads, to his shed, where he drank a warm beer and tried to distract himself by viewing photographs of naked women in his magazines, but even those rosy nipples reminded him of the dummy's burning eyes. There was only one thing to do, he finally admitted.

While it would be impossible for him to return the bike he had stolen because it was long gone, he could steal another, a better one, and give it to that kid. It would get him off Lamar's back at last, and nobody else had to know. Feeling relieved at having made the decision, the fat boy opened a second beer. There would be nothing to it; the only dangerous part would be sneaking off the yard without his daddy catching him.

The following Saturday, Lamar turned on the radio beside his bed, locked his door from the inside, then crawled out the window and headed for the River Theater where kids would be watching the matinee, and where a selection of unlocked bicycles could always be found. He strolled casually by the bike rack, skillfully assessing the merchandise out the corner of his eye, since he didn't want the lady in the box office to notice him. For several minutes Lamar appeared to be studying the posters of coming attractions when, in fact, he was scrutinizing a luxurious Schwinn. He would present Bertil with a model so good that the dummy would never again bother him.

Finally, after searching up and down the street, he zeroed in on the box office lady, waiting until she was distracted. A few minutes later, the telephone rang and she began talking. Lamar strolled casually to the shining Schwinn, slipped it from the rack, and rode for the nearest corner. There was nothing to it.

Pedaling toward Bertil's ramshackle house, Lamar considered how to present the gift. He couldn't afford to give the impression he was frightened or desperate or anything like that; he was, after all, Lamar Studly, toughest kid in the sixth grade. But if he acted too rough, he might scare the dummy and prolong his own misery. It was a dilemma. He decided finally to be humble and direct but not friendly, to let the runt know this was a favor. He didn't owe the dummy anything, but even the toughest kid in the class could be kind. As satisfying as that resolution was, a nagging doubt remained in Lamar's ample middle: what if the dummy refused to accept the bike? No, he wouldn't do that, he couldn't.

And he didn't. Bertil was sitting on his rickety porch preparing for his paper route, rolling newspapers and placing rubber bands around them, then stuffing them into his canvas bag. Two younger brothers and sisters were browsing over their dirt yard, and another was talking to a lady in the next yard. It was perfect for Lamar, who stopped in the street and climbed off the shining bicycle. Before Bertil could speak, Lamar pushed the Schwinn up to the porch and announced, "You can deliver your papers on this here."

Bertil's little red eyes searched the lovely Schwinn, examined it minutely. Lamar was ready with a lie dummy asked where it came from, but he didn't. Instead, he stood up in that odd, crooked way of his, walked to the bicycle and gripped its handlebars. Lamar released the bike and Bertil stood holding his new Schwinn. It was better than Lamar had imagined because the smaller boy appeared to be speechless. Elated by this happy turn, the fat boy said, "Thank you, Lamar," as sarcastically as he could, but Bertil ignored him.

"I don't wanna hear no more about that other bike from you," Lamar advised harshly, "or I'll come back and take thisun away and you won't have nothin'."

Bertil's face was sliced by a mysterious smile, but he remained silent.

The fat boy waited a moment longer for a response, but finally shrugged: what can you expect from a kid in the retard class that lives in this dump, he thought. At least I'm shed of him. After pulling out a pocket comb and rearranging his dark, oily hair, the toughest kid in the sixth grade turned and, without saying goodbye, began his trek home at a livelier strut than he'd managed for a long time.

Feverish eyes locked on the stout figure swaggering away, then Bertil whispered, "*Now* I got na evinence," and his visionary smile widened. "I *got* na evinence."

Flesh and Blood

See what's carved on that old poplar? *Mar-3-27.* I did that myself the night of the big lynching. I was young then just like the tree—we've both gnarled some since—and I was fired by whiskey and righteous white man's indignation, so I carved the date right there while Cousin Charlie Hughes and Shorty Gireaux took turns hollering at us boys to stir us up. I wanted that night to be remembered.

Not that us boys needed much hollering. We were plenty hot to start with, see. I mean, one jigaboo in town and he turns out to be uppity. Well, we were plenty able to handle that little problem, as Mr. Moses Moore was about to find out. Cousin Charlie had brought a rope, which was only fair since it was his youngster the jig had abused.

See, Bud, Charlie's oldest, was captain of the Wildcats and a real pistol. I guess he was about the best high school football player in the valley, that boy. His daddy was surely proud of him. That's why he—Cousin Charlie, I mean— stirred up the necktie party after that coon abused poor Bud.

You may wonder how come a colored settled here in the first place, what with this being an oil town and all. Well, you don't wonder more than most of us, I'll tell you. The darkie first came to the westside from down south with a troop of prize fighters, and he whipped his fair share of roughnecks from Maricopa to Coalinga for the next couple of years.

He wasn't a spring chicken then, and he wasn't too large, about medium size I'd say, but he was handy. He took on all comers and usually settled things real quick. Anyway, he finally ran into a big, tough Basque over in Bakersfield and took a pretty hard pounding, though I'm told he won the fight. A month or so later he opened a shine stand downtown next to Abe Goldschmidt's Tonsorial Parlor.

There were a lot of us respectable citizens who let Abe know we didn't appreciate it, too.

At the time, there was talk about running the coon out of town, but he was friendly and didn't bother anyone, so we let it slide. That's where we made our mistake. We thought he knew his place, see.

Still, I don't understand why he stayed in town. I mean, if he had any social life it must have revolved around the colored section over in Bakersfield where he spent a weekend every month. Other than that, I'd never see him anywhere but at his stand or sitting in the back of the First Christian Church on Sunday or, and I'm a little ashamed to admit this, sitting out on our front porch talking to Uncle A.J.

In some ways, maybe, it wasn't entirely the nigger's fault that Bud got roughed up. The kid was frisky, see, and when he lunged past the bootblack and threw a jar of liquid polish at young Jimmy Dalby, who was having his shoes spiffed up at the time, he not only bumped Moses pretty good, but he half-knocked over his stand too. Still, you have to draw the line on coloreds somewhere, and what followed went way past the limit.

Now I didn't see it, but I've heard several stories and they all agree that the jig gave the boy a licking, not whipping him man-to-man, but licking him man-to-child right there on Main Street. Cousin Charlie wasn't standing for that, I'll tell you. He closed his hardware store soon as he heard and headed for The Cable Tool Saloon.

It just so happens I was there when Charlie busted in, spitting nickels he was so mad. Word spread fast, and by dusk there were roustabouts and roughnecks streaming in from Fellows to McKittrick, all of them hot to hang a nigger. Me, I wouldn't've missed it for anything.

I rushed home from The Cable Tool and hurried through the house telling everyone what the nigger'd done and urging them to come to the hanging. "What?" barked Uncle A.J. when he heard me, and he didn't sound very happy. I wasn't surprised. Uncle A.J., my mother's brother, was the town do-gooder, a book-learning and turn-your-other-cheek Christian, deacon of the church and city attorney. He thought he was better than the rest of us just because he'd gone away to the university, but I knew better, see. I knew he was about two balls short of being a real man, with his soft talk and nigger-loving ways. No way he'd be up to a hanging.

"That spade bootblack of yours beat up on little Bud Hughes. We're stringing him up."

Uncle A.J. eyed me and I thought for a minute he wasn't going to reply. "You're what?" he finally asked.

"Stringing his uppity black ass up!"

Again there was a long pause. "Are you talking about Moses Moore?"

"I'm not talking about Jack Johnson!" Me, I liked to come up with snappy answers.

"Moses is a Christian and a gentleman. He doesn't bother anyone, though Lord knows he's had reason enough to throttle some of the weevils he's had to put up with."

"That's what you say!" I spat. "He's attacked one white child too many and we're gonna settle his hash, see!" I slammed out the screen door and headed for the poplar in the town square. I'd heard enough from a nigger lover, uncle or no uncle.

But A.J. wasn't through talking. I should've expected that he'd show up and defend the coon, because I knew for a fact that he not only talked with him, but loaned him books and one time even advanced him money. I'd even seen the two of them shake hands, so what could you expect?

Shorty Gireaux was up on a wagon preaching to us, see, when A.J. appeared and cut through the crowd directly to its core, then ordered Shorty to climb down. Shorty obeyed. Uncle A.J. was a little-bitty man with no more muscle than a worm, but his education awed most of the boys. If they didn't want a fist fight with Moses Moore, they wanted a tongue lashing from my uncle even less.

Up on the wagon, A.J. stood with one hand holding a lapel and the other gesturing just like he did in court, but his voice rang higher and hotter than usual. "You boys hold on!" he demanded. "Look at yourselves all liquored up and foolish. What is this?"

100

Several of the boys from out of town ventured answers, but he ignored them. "You've all known Moses for years," he continued. "He's polished your boots and run your errands and not a man jack of you's ever had any trouble from him, have you?" He paused while some in the crowd murmured assent, then added, "Even when *you* were out of line." More boys nodded and turned to speak softly to one another. A scrawny guy next to me said, "That's right," as though he'd never thought of it before.

I didn't like the way things were turning, I'll tell you, and I was about to say something when Cousin Charlie's voice roared from the crowd. "He hurt my little boy, that's what he done! Don't let him get away with that!"

"Yeah! Yeah!" I shouted, and so did most of the crowd.

A.J. waited until we all quieted some before he spoke again, but when he did he almost got shot by Cousin Charlie, who I knew was carrying a pistol, see. "How big's that *little* boy of yours, Charlie? Six-foot? Six-foot-two? What's he dress out? Two hundred? Two-ten?"

"God damnit!" roared Charlie, and I saw him go for that big revolver. Fortunately, a couple of older men, both drillers, were standing near him and they grabbed him before he could get a round off. They knew as surely as I did if he'd shot A.J. the state would've hung him. Those lawyers stick together, see.

Even though he saw the scuffle in the crowd, and I'm sure he knew what was happening, A.J. kept talking. "That poor innocent victim isn't the kid who's caused such devilment here-abouts, is he? Shorty," he called to Charlie's best friend. "Who was it you said ought to be horsewhipped after the picnic last fall?" Shorty looked at his boots. "Melville," A.J. shouted to a merchant who stood near me in the crowd, "what was it you said ought to be clipped after Bud bothered your girls last summer?" No response. "And you, Gerald," my own name startled me, "who did you say would end up in the penitentiary if he didn't change his ways?" Now that really made me sore, see, him repeating what I'd said, and doing it right in front of Cousin Charlie.

My whiskey was turning sour. In fact, I think everyone's was. A.J. had taken the fun out of things. I felt like going home. Then, like magic, Charlie's wife Isabel materialized on the other side of the crowd and, in a voice thick with tears, she cried, "A.J. Graham, I'm ashamed of you. You talk about my son that way. You let a nigger beat him half-to-death and go unpunished. Seems like the nigger means more to you than your own flesh and blood! What's next? Do us womenfolk have to stay indoors from now on? I want you men, you real men, to do something! I want . . ." She collapsed into loud sobs, unable to continue. There was considerable din after that, but I heard A.J. respond, "Justice, Isabel, justice means more than my own flesh and blood." But nobody paid him any mind, see, because Cousin Charlie, disarmed now, took up where his wife had stopped.

"You boys let a coon attack a white kid and get away with it, and white women'll be next. If you want that African bastard slobberin' all over your wives and daughters that's your business, but me, I'm teachin' him a lesson!"

That quickly the crowd was ready for action again, and A.J. seemed to sense the danger in trying to stop them. In fact, I thought he might get his own neck stretched and, after the way he'd embarrassed me, I wouldn't have helped him, relative or not. Still, he would not relent. This time his voice roared. "You can't kill a man for what he might do! If that was the case there's plenty in this crowd who'd be swinging right now." Few were paying A.J. any mind until he said, "And every man jack who's involved in a lynching in my jurisdiction will hang. That's a promise."

He meant it, there was no question, and the crowd quieted again, milling restlessly, but unwilling to follow Cousin Charlie who had started for Moses Moore's cabin, then stopped when his allies deserted him. We were torn between the need to protect our women and children, especially our women, since there were so few of them in the oil camps, and the fact that Uncle A.J. could enforce his threat.

Then Cousin Charlie had screamed, his voice raw and desperate, "We can't let the jigaboo get away with it!" Uncle A.J. jumped in with a proposal it sounded like he'd been hoarding the whole time. "If we have to do something, then let's at least be sensible. The first one of us who crosses Moses's path tomorrow is to give him a good whipping, which is all he did to Bud. If it stops there, I'll see that no charges are lodged. A beating will keep him in his place, and it'll keep you on the right side of the law. Beat him with your fists only!"

Rumbles of agreement stirred the crowd, most of whom had lost their stomach for lynching when A.J. promised to hang them. Immediately, clusters of men began moving off, talking among themselves. There was one small problem, though, one most of the crowd missed because of their relief and their whiskey: none of us could whip Moses. It was something we never talked about, but we all knew it and were ashamed. Before the crowd had totally broken up, I decided I'd find work to do at home the next day.

And I did, puttering around all morning, careful to stay inside even though I knew I'd have to face Uncle A.J. sooner or later unless I left. Besides, I wasn't feeling too good anyway, what with my head hurting and all, so I conspired to stay in my own room as much as I could without looking yellow.

Uncle A.J. came down to breakfast a little later than usual, about mid-morning, see. I gave him a wide berth, but I kept my eye on him all the same. Once he was finished eating, he walked into the hallway, put on his Stetson and adjusted his coat and tie before the mirror, then strolled out onto the porch to walk to his office. But he didn't get far. Moses Moore stood at the foot of the porch steps.

Soon as I saw the darkie I scrambled out the back door and hurried around the house, then positioned myself behind the big pyracantha next to the porch. I don't think either man had spoken before I arrived. Uncle A.J. stood on the top step and Moses on the walkway below him, each looking straight at the other. Finally, the bootblack said, "I heard what you did last night and I'm beholden to you."

As was usual with my uncle, he paused before answering. I figured it had all been a plan between them, so I half expected them to sit together on the porch swing and discuss philosophy and all, but they didn't. Uncle A.J. sighed. "You know what I've got to do, don't you, Moses?" he said finally.

"I know."

Uncle A.J. carefully removed his coat and folded it over the porch railing, placed his hat on top of it, then descended the steps until he stood directly in front of the coon. Without a word, he balled one small fist and drew it back and punched Moses Moore flush on the mouth, snapping his head back. Before the nigger could recover, A.J. hit him once more, then a third time, then a fourth, each with surprising force, while Moses made no effort to defend himself.

The darkie's lip was split and trickling blood and one of his eyes was watery and blinking. I had been astounded at the fury of Uncle A.J.'s attack and I forgot what he'd done the night before as my own blood came up. Just as my uncle cocked his right fist again, Moses said, "That's enough." It wasn't a request or a concession, just a statement, so I leaped from behind the bush to help Uncle A.J. finish teaching the nigger a lesson. "Damn jig," I snarled.

A.J.'s eyes snapped toward me. They were cold as a valley rattler's. In an instant he gripped my collar so tightly that he choked me. "You use that word in my presence again and I'll wear you out," he hissed. He released me and I staggered back a step.

"Moses Moore has had his beating," Uncle A.J. declared. "You spread the word to your saloon friends. And you tell them that the next man jack who lays a hand on him will deal with the law of the State of California."

"You . . ." I sputtered, still in shock, see, "you wait'll Cousin Charlie hears . . ."

A.J. cut me off. "I've already seen to Charlie Hughes," he growled. "Now get in the house." I obeyed. I mean I'd never seen him act like that before and I was more than a little scared, what with his nigger friend there to back him up and all. I'd seen that same animal danger in the darkie's eyes I'd seen in A.J.'s.

So that was it, the big lynching, see. And, yep, it was me that carved on the poplar. I was half-tempted to go scratch the whole damn thing off but I never got around to it. I guess it doesn't really matter anyway. Nothing important ever happens around here.

My Dear Mr. Thorp

Feb. 3, 1985

My Dear Mr. Thorp:

The world will soon end unless human beings begin to love one another in God's fullness. Thusly, I am submitting to you the enclosed three brief poems celebrating our Oneness with the Eternal. Please note the subtle symbolism and the lyric qualities found in each. As the enclosed resume indicates, I have been widely published in the PIXLEY DAILY RECORD and the TRUE BIBLE CHURCH BULLETIN. It is time, however, for my inspirational poems to reach a national audience and I have chosen your journal THE ATWOOD REVIEW to carry the message. If you do a good job with these poems, I have others I might send to you. I hope you enjoy the newspaper articles I enclose, plus the Zeroxed page from WHO'S WHO IN THE TRUE BIBLE CHURCH. *All three of these poems are copyrighted to me.* I also enclose a stamped, self-addressed envelope. I am looking forward to your prompt reply.

Sincerely yours,

J. Elbert Duggan (poet)

Feb. 7, 1985

Dear Mr. Duggan:

Thank you for submitting your work to *The Atwood*

Review. While it does not suit our present needs, we do wish you the best of luck placing it elsewhere.

With best wishes,

Roger Thorp, editor
The Atwood Review

Feb. 10, 1985

My Dear Mr. Thorp:

Perhaps there has been a mistake. The three poems I sent to you, "Pixley Agonistis," "Heaven Found," and "God's Messenger," have been widely praised as being among my best. Did you confuse them with someone else's? If so, I am still willing to allow you to publish them. They are, by the way, *copyrighted to me,* just in case somebody on your staff has any ideas.

Sincerely yours,

J. Elbert Duggan (poet)

Feb., 21, 1985

My Dear Mr. Thorp:

Since you have not had the courtesy to answer my last letter, I must assume that I have misjudged you. I have today spoken to Attorney Randle McQuaid informing him of the possible abuse of my copyrights by members of your staff. We will be watching you closely. Attorney McQuaid is also a member of the True Bible Church.

Sincerely yours,

J. Elbert Duggan (poet)

Feb. 21, 1985

Dear editors:

THE BARD HATH LONG SINCE
GRIPPED MY HEART,
SO WITH THESE PRECIOUS LINES
I PART.

ENCLOSED WITH POEMS
YOU WILL FIND
NOT ONLY S.A.S.E.
BUT TIES THAT BIND.

PRAY, DEAR SIR, DO
READ WITH LOVE,
THESE LINES INSPIRED
FROM ABOVE.

Yours for poetry,

Marjorie Marie Rampetti

Feb. 26, 1985

Dear Ms. Rampetti:

Thank you for submitting your work to *The Atwood Review*. While it does not suit our present needs, we do wish you the best of luck placing it elsewhere.

With best wishes,

Roger Thorp, editor
The Atwood Review

March 1, 1983

Dear Mr. Thorp:

Please consider the enclosed poem, "Wolf's Cry," for publication in *The Atwood Review*. You are, of course, familiar with my work. As a matter of form, however, I enclose S.A.S.E.

Sincerely,

Morgan Jackson

March 12, 1985

Dear Mr. Jackson:

Thank you for submitting your work to *The Atwood*

Review. While it does not suit our present needs, we do wish you the best of luck placing it elsewhere.

With best wishes,

Roger Thorp, editor
The Atwood Review

March 20, 1985

Dear male:

Here is your chance to undo thousands of years of oppression of Wimin. Are you enlightened enough to allow the truth to be proclaimed? You will note that we have moved beyond the old, male-dominated word "wo (like halt)-man." We have also moved beyond male imposed sexual roles. Thus the enclosed manifesto: "Personhood!"

For all of history in the supposed "civilized" west the small differences between the sexes have been exaggerated by exploiting males, who created a slave-class of Wimin. Males in sciences such as endocrinology, medicine, and sociobiology have sought to create the illusion that men and Wimin are essentially different. IT'S A LIE!

"Personhood!" reveals the whole rotten conspiracy. Here is your chance to participate in the new consciousness that will liberate all people. Are *you* liberated enough to publish it?

Solidarity Forever!

Patsy Ross
Charleston Feminist Collective

March 29, 1985

Dear Ms. Ross:

Thank you for submitting your work to *The Atwood Review*. While it does not suit our present needs, we do wish you the best of luck placing it elsewhere. Please send S.A.S.E. so I can return your manuscript.

With best wishes,

Roger Thorp, editor
The Atwood Review

April 5, 1985

Pig Thorp:

You revealed yourself! Your name is on our list! RETURN OUR MANIFESTO, PIG!

Patsy Ross
Charleston Feminist Collective

April 9, 1985

PIG THORP:

THIS IS YOUR LAST WARNING! RETURN OUR MANIFESTO!

PATSY ROSS & C.F.C.

April 28, 1985

Dear Sir:

I've never wrote anything before, but here's a poem that makes the boys at the bar where I hang out laugh.

About me—no poet, just a regular guy. Born in Oklahoma in 1937. Fell in the glory hole of an outhouse in 1939. Never been the same. My folks, after some argument, decided to clean me up and keep me. I sold newspapers and once smoked a Tampax—like one long filter. I sold crickets to fishermen and ate a couple—crickets, not fishermen—just to see why the fish bit—tasted pretty fair. Also ate a worm and a dragonfly—stick with crickets if you get the chance. Played doctor with the girl across the street in 1948, and '49, and '50, and so on. Better than crickets. Went to high school and even graduated. Tried smoking in 1952—quit in 1953—tasted like shit. Arrested for painting pubic hair on all statues in city park. Went on the road in '55 and worked dipping seed potatoes and waitresses in Utah. Packed grapes and waitresses in California. Army '57-'59—prefer crickets or waitresses. Back on the road, drinking a little beer, then a lot. Tried dope, also drugs. Played doctor some more—better all the time. Thinned sugar beets, picked potatoes, tended bar, rode rails. Back to crickets. And waitresses. Married a cute one—waitress, not cricket—in '62. Stole a car and didn't get caught. Dipped snuff. Settled down and worked in a feed store. Played doctor with lady that also worked there. Back on the road in '66. (To be continued—life, not letter)

So here's the poem. Hope you like it but I enclose some stamps. Do not smoke them.

Cheers,

Rapid City Robert

May 4, 1985

Dear Robert:

Your poem is lousy. I'd like to publish your letter, however. What do you say?

With best wishes,

Roger Thorp, editor
The Atwood Review

P.S. About that girl you played doctor with—was her name Patsy Ross?

May 12, 1985

Dear Sir:

Hell yeah, print what you want. No, it wasn't Patsy, but send me her address and I'll see what I can do. Don't feel bad about the poem. I stole it anyway.

Cheers,

Rapid City Robert

May 14, 1985

Roger Thorp, Editor
Atwood Review
Box 102
Atwood, Calif. 94900

Dear Mr. Thorp:

I am sending you three poems in the hope that one may be acceptable for publication in *Atwood Review*. It would be a great honor to be published in your pages since it is a truly great journal and it has always been my very favorite. Please do not think because I am sending you photocopies that I am also sending them to any other journal. It is just that I like to keep the originals in my files.

Well, Mr. Thorp, it is up to you. You can make a poet very happy by honoring him with publication in your great journal. Won't you please?

Very truly yours,

Lauren Lafayette (pen name)
Bill Schwartz (real name)

May 19, 1985

Roger Thorp, Editor
Atwood Review
Box 102
Atwood, Calif. 94900

Dear Mr. Thorp:

Never mind the poems I sent you. They are being published elsewhere. How long did you think I would wait?

Very truly yours,

Lauren Lafayette (pen name)
Bill Schwartz (real name)

June 7, 1985

Dear Mr. Thorp:

Well, I'm in love again, as the enclosed poems show. I hope they also show some hint of talent and craft. Being realistic, I enclose S.A.S.E.; being optimistic, I hope you don't use it. Thanks in advance for your time.

Yours hopefully,

Rita Lou Bowen

June 14, 1985

Dear Ms. Bowen:

It will be our pleasure to publish your sensitive, original poetry. We all thought the subject had been exhausted, but you have proven us wrong. Thanks.

I will be sending you galley proofs in about three months.

With best wishes,

Roger Thorp, editor
The Atwood Review

July 1, 1985

My Dear Mr. Thorp:

Since your thoughtless rejection of my poetry, I have sent it to nine other magazines and all have sent it back. There can only be one reason for this—you contacted other editors and used your influence to convince them not to publish my poems. Well, you have made the wrong enemy. I have discussed this matter with Attorney Randle McQuaid and he assures me that your behavior is *actionable*. You have not heard the last of me.

Sincerely yours,

J. Elbert Duggan (poet)

Snapshots

Velma Marie had her snapshots, thank heaven. At least she had them. On quiet evenings when none of her programs were coming on, she'd sit at the dinette table and stare into the past, turning the heavy black pages of her photo albums, gazing at gray yesterdays, their corners wedged into four tiny triangles.

"My lord," she sighed, "look at Myrtle in that bathin' suit." Then she chuckled.

"Sometimes I think you've went nuts," Sam groused loudly from the living room where he was reading the newspaper. "It sounds like you're talkin' to them pitchers again."

"Oh, hush," she chuckled. It was an old game between them. He was just jealous, she knew, because he never could take a decent photograph. His always looked like thumbprints. But she took clear ones, and it never ceased to amaze her what she could do with a small camera: conquer time with a single touch.

Sam, poor Sam, was time's captive, incapable of being more than he was at the moment. He disliked photos, apparently finding pain in what he thought was a lost past. He didn't even look at his old football pictures. On the other hand, Velma Marie with her snapshots was the sum of herself.

In the green album, she touched Gerald when he was just a baby, him giggling and cooing at his momma. Such a cute little bundle, and to think he was a father himself now. She picked up another album and turned to a photo of her grandson, Ronnie Ray. My, my . . ..

"What're you laughin' at?" Sam called.

"You, you old fool!" She'd get him told is what she'd do, chuckling louder. It was so much fun to see everyone.

"Humph," was his only response.

Funny thing is, it was Sam himself who had bought her that first camera, a little Kodak, way back .when they were dating. And what joy it had been to dress up and mug, or to talk Hazel and Earl into hugging, or to pose with that old colored man who shined shoes, and she had all those memories mounted forever, waiting in her albums.

She opened the red one and there stood Hazel and Earl. "Oh, kid," Velma Marie chided, "I seen what you two was doin' under that willow."

"You *did* not," Hazel insisted.

"Oh yes I did."

"You *did* not. Besides, it's none of your beeswax anyways," snapped Hazel.

"Ooo-la-la!" winked Velma Marie.

Earl, who said nothing, only grinned that peppery grin of his and it told her there sure enough had been something to see, even if she really hadn't seen it.

"I wonder how Earl's doin'?" she called into the next room.

"Hell, he's had it," Sam responded. "That cancer's got him bad. The doc says he can't last a month. I went by and seen him yesterday."

Poor Hazel struggling with emphysema, and now Earl. She stared hard into the frozen photo faces. "Oh, kid," she said to Hazel, "you *had* to smoke those darn cigarettes."

"Mind your own beeswax," snapped Hazel, always quick with her tongue.

"Oh, *you*," Velma Marie said, shaking her head.

"What?" called Sam.

"I wasn't speakin' to you," she informed him.

"You better stop that talkin' to yourself before somebody puts you in the nuthouse."

"You better just watch out yourself!" she snapped. Then she returned to Hazel. "I'll tell you, kid, I never thought Sam'd be such a *grouch* when I married him."

"Well, of course not," Hazel pointed out, "all you seen was them shoulders and that letter sweater."

"I *did* not."

"Did so."

"I *did* not."

There was no arguing with her, so Velma Marie let it go. She turned her attention toward Earl, standing with his tanned arms around the girl who would be his wife, straw cowboy hat pushed back on his head so that a carefully placed curl fell across his forehead. She searched his face, that impish grin, those saucy eyes—full of the old Ned is what he was—intent on what hid there: the drawn, discolored mask she had herself seen just last week, the pained, bewildered eyes.

She flipped the page and beheld Madge in the waitress uniform she had worn at Woolworth's, and so proud too: she had the *cutest* figure. Velma Marie and Momma had marched right down there and ordered B.L.T.'s that very first day so they could see her behind the counter. Madge waved shyly and snapped her chewing gum.

On the next page stood Helen Rose in her graduation gown, looking almost like a queen. The entire family had turned out for that, the youngest daughter graduating from high school, and giving a speech too: "But we must be mindful of the world we enter," Helen Rose said, "for our childhoods have ended."

"What's that?" called Sam.

"She wasn't talkin' to *you*," his wife retorted, then returned her attention to her younger sister's speech: "Ours is the responsibility of building a better society. Ours is the responsibility of making the world free and safe. Ours is the responsibility of seeing that God is not forgotten."

Velma Marie sighed. It was so stirring is what it was. "That was real good, honey," she told her little sister, who dimpled, then bowed her head. How could a shy girl like her stand up and give a speech? I swan!

Donnie Hardin could give speeches too. Oh my lord, Donnie. She turned slowly to her one small, gray photograph of him, taken in the carnival photo booth at the fair. Unmoving, Donnie grinned, his freckles hardly showing, his thin shoulders hunched up like he was cold. He'd always looked like a poor little orphan child, so skinny and all, but smart as a whip.

Sam had been out of town with the football team that night when Velma Marie and Donnie had attended the fair, that night when they had danced at the pavilion, that night when they had wandered together to the levee and sat in the warm darkness listening to the Kern River slide by. That night when she had leaned forward and kissed Donnie and he, after a moment of hesitation, had kissed back. When they had both kissed.

"Oh, Donnie," she whispered, "it's us again." Her voice thickened, her eyes warmed, and she gazed at the small portrait.

Donnie said nothing, as he had said nothing that night. Velma Marie's breath quickened and deep within herself something surged. Again she murmured, "Oh, Donnie." The photo remained mute. He usually said little, but what he said always mattered. His silence tonight troubled her.

Well, it served her right. Donnie had been the first, the only other than Sam, who had been the second. She could have broken up with Sam after that night, but she had tried to hold them both. Donnie would have none of it. Finally, she had to have her football hero, so she chose Sam. Velma Marie had him then, and the grieving eyes of Donnie Hardin whenever they met. It had been her fault, no denying it. Tears welled as she gazed at the carnival portrait in her album.

When she had finally allowed Sam to touch her as Donnie had, her football star had to brag to his teammates about it. He probably wouldn't even have married her if she hadn't become pregnant. Donnie, she knew, never told anyone. She knew because of the message in his eyes even now, and because of the tender kiss he had left on her cheek after her wedding. She knew because this silent photograph had once told her so.

"You read this?" Sam called.

She cleared her throat. "Read what?"

"You remember that Hardin kid that went to school with us, the one that used to make moon-eyes at you?"

Her eyes fled momentarily to the silent photo before her, then she replied, "Yes."

"Well, he died. In Albuquerque. Says he was a lawyer. Huh! He couldn't even make the team."

"He what?"

"He couldn't even make the damn team."

"No," she cried, "before that! What'd you say before that?"

Sam lurched into the doorway. "What the hell's wrong with you?"

"He what?" Velma Marie demanded.

"Kicked the bucket is what," Sam spat, then he returned to the living room.

"Passed away," she moaned to herself, and her hand moved slowly until it covered the tiny portrait. Her other hand touched the cheek where once she'd felt that tender kiss. Slowly, softly—just as she had that night on the levee—Velma Marie leaned forward and kissed Donnie one last time. When she opened her eyes, his face was gone, replaced by a smudge, and her lips were touched with gray powder.

Still staring at the smudged portrait, she stood, plucked it from the black page, and held it gently in one damp palm. Then she retreated to her bed and folded her heavy body into the slim space it had long ago occupied, pleated it around Donnie. There in the deepest dark she had ever known, she sighed and touched her tongue to her lips, to the bitter dust covering her lips.

About the Author

GERALD HASLAM is a native of Oildale, a small town in the Bakersfield area of California's San Joaquin Valley. As a boy, he labored in that region's farms and packing sheds. Later, after a stint in the army, he worked as a roustabout and roughneck in the oil fields to put himself through college. He was educated at Bakersfield Junior College, San Francisco State College, Washington State University, and the Union for Experimenting Colleges and Universities.

Perhaps more than those of any other contemporary fiction writer, Haslam's stories explore the California ignored by the golden state's stereotype. His writing features small-town hoods, country musicians, migrant laborers, and aging cowhands; Asians, Latinos, Blacks, and Indians, as well as all varieties of Whites. He sets his stories in the state's vast central valley and coastal ranges, in its northern woodlands and eastern deserts, in trailer parks and junk yards, tract homes and beer bars.

Haslam's first short-story collection, *Okies*, appeared in 1973; it remains in print in a third edition. His first and so-far lone novel, *Masks*, was published three years later. *The Wages of Sin*, another collection of tales, was released in 1980, and *Hawk Flights: Visions of the West*, one more collection of stories, appeared in 1983. His short fiction has been widely anthologized. He has also published a number of non-fiction titles including *Forgotten Pages of American Literature* (1970), *Western Writing* (1974), and *California Heartland* (with James D. Houston, 1978).

Haslam continues to live in California, where he teaches at Sonoma State University. His work is the subject of a forthcoming booklet written by Gerald Locklin for the Western Writers Series, and was recently the topic of an honors humanities thesis at Stanford University.